STONE ARCH BOOKS
a capstone imprint

STONE ARCH BOOKS™

Published in 2012
A Capstone Imprint
1710 Roe Crest Drive
North Mankato, MN 56003
www.capstonepub.com

Originally published by DC Comics in the U.S. in single magazine form as Batman Adventures #2.

DC Comics
1700 Broadway, New York, NY 10019
A Warner Bros. Entertainment Company

Printed and bound in China by Nordica.
112013 007892R
1213/CA21302219

Cataloging-in-Publication Data is available at the Library of Congress website:
ISBN: 978-1-4342-4558-8 (library binding)

Summary: Hunted mercilessly by shadow assassins, The Riddler turns to Batman for help. But even a Riddler on good behavior can't resist playing games with the Dark Knight.

STONE ARCH BOOKS

Ashley C. Andersen Zantop *Publisher*
Michael Dahl *Editorial Director*
Donald Lemke & Sean Tulien *Editors*
Heather Kindseth *Creative Director*
Bob Lentz *Designer*
Kathy McColley *Production Specialist*

DC COMICS

Joan Hilty *Original U.S. Editor*
Harvey Richards *U.S. Assistant Editor*
Bruce Timm *Cover Artist*

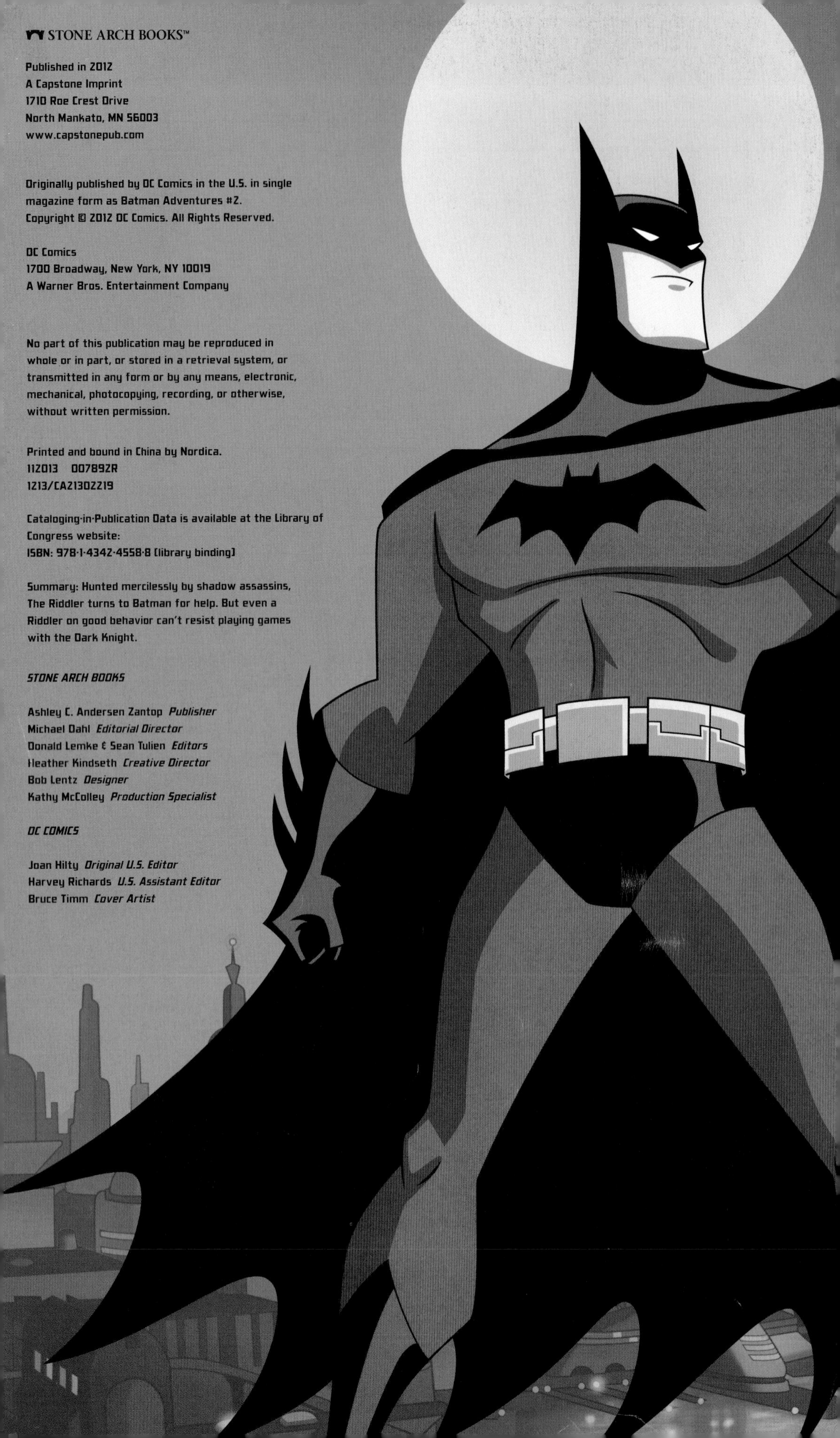

BATMAN ADVENTURES

FREE MAN

Ty Templeton & Dan Slott .... writers
Rick Burchett & Ty Templeton .... pencillers
Terry Beatty .... inker
Lee Loughridge & Zylonol Studios .... colorists
Phil Felix .... letterer

**Batman created by
Bob Kane**

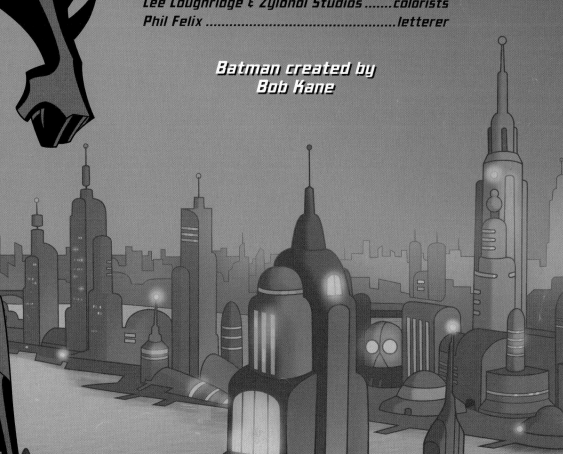

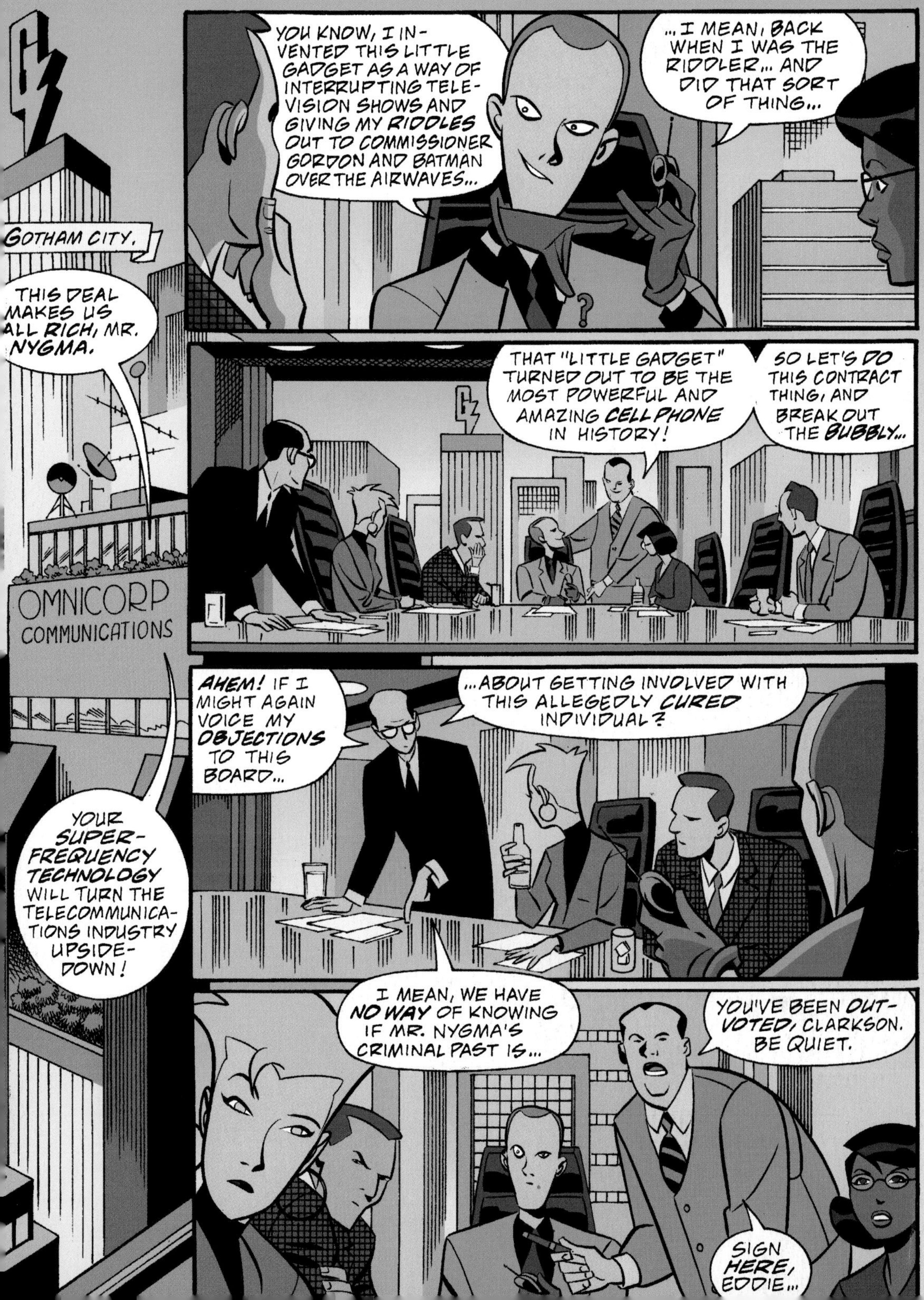
GOTHAM CITY.
THIS DEAL MAKES US ALL RICH, MR. NYGMA.
YOU KNOW, I INVENTED THIS LITTLE GADGET AS A WAY OF INTERRUPTING TELEVISION SHOWS AND GIVING MY RIDDLES OUT TO COMMISSIONER GORDON AND BATMAN OVER THE AIRWAVES...
...I MEAN, BACK WHEN I WAS THE RIDDLER... AND DID THAT SORT OF THING...
OMNICORP COMMUNICATIONS
THAT "LITTLE GADGET" TURNED OUT TO BE THE MOST POWERFUL AND AMAZING CELL PHONE IN HISTORY!
SO LET'S DO THIS CONTRACT THING, AND BREAK OUT THE BUBBLY...
YOUR SUPER-FREQUENCY TECHNOLOGY WILL TURN THE TELECOMMUNICATIONS INDUSTRY UPSIDE-DOWN!
AHEM! IF I MIGHT AGAIN VOICE MY OBJECTIONS TO THIS BOARD...
...ABOUT GETTING INVOLVED WITH THIS ALLEGEDLY CURED INDIVIDUAL?
I MEAN, WE HAVE NO WAY OF KNOWING IF MR. NYGMA'S CRIMINAL PAST IS...
YOU'VE BEEN OUT-VOTED, CLARKSON. BE QUIET.
SIGN HERE, EDDIE...

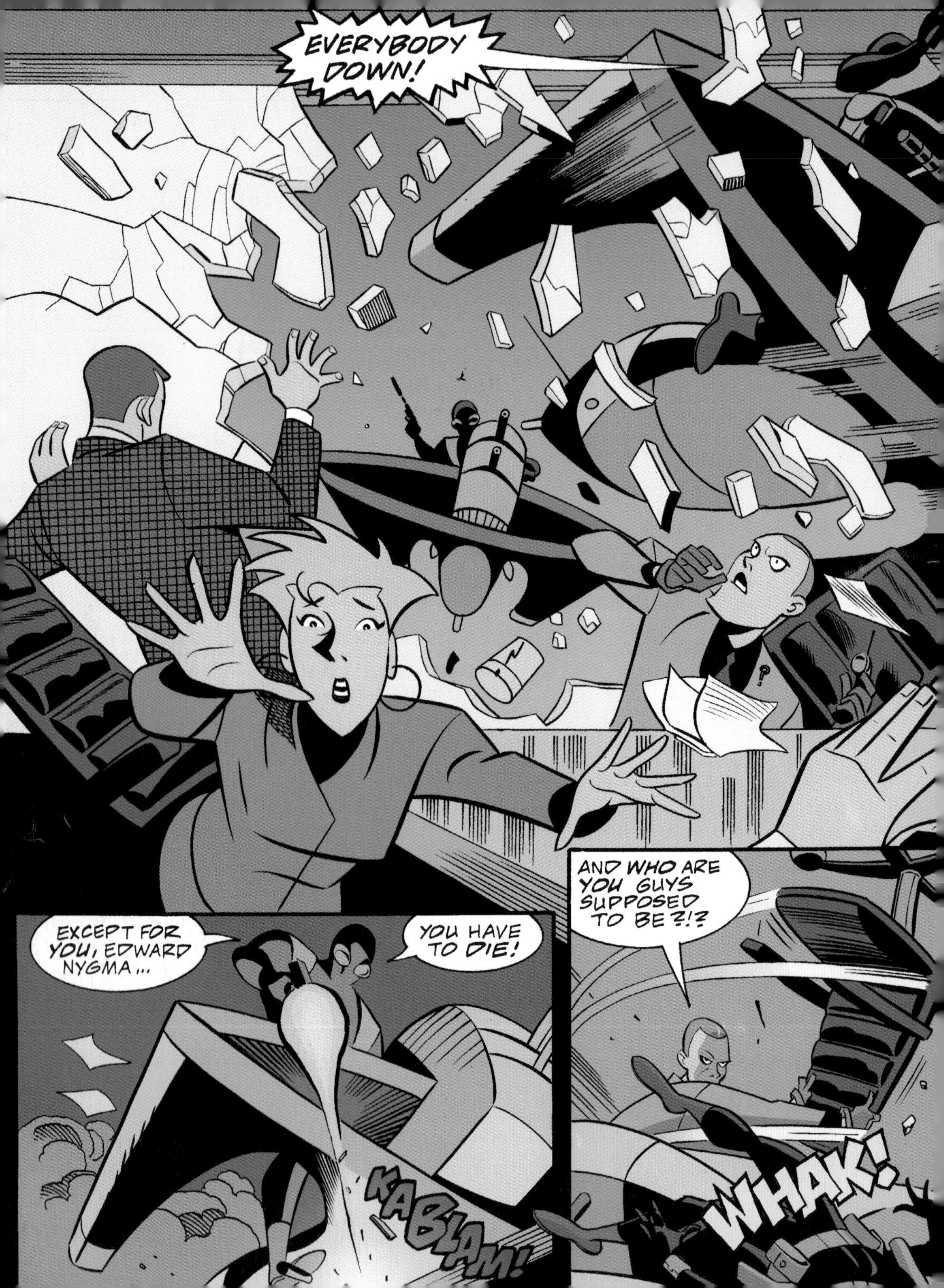
EVERYBODY DOWN!
EXCEPT FOR YOU, EDWARD NYGMA...
YOU HAVE TO DIE!
KABLAM!
AND WHO ARE YOU GUYS SUPPOSED TO BE?!?
WHAK!

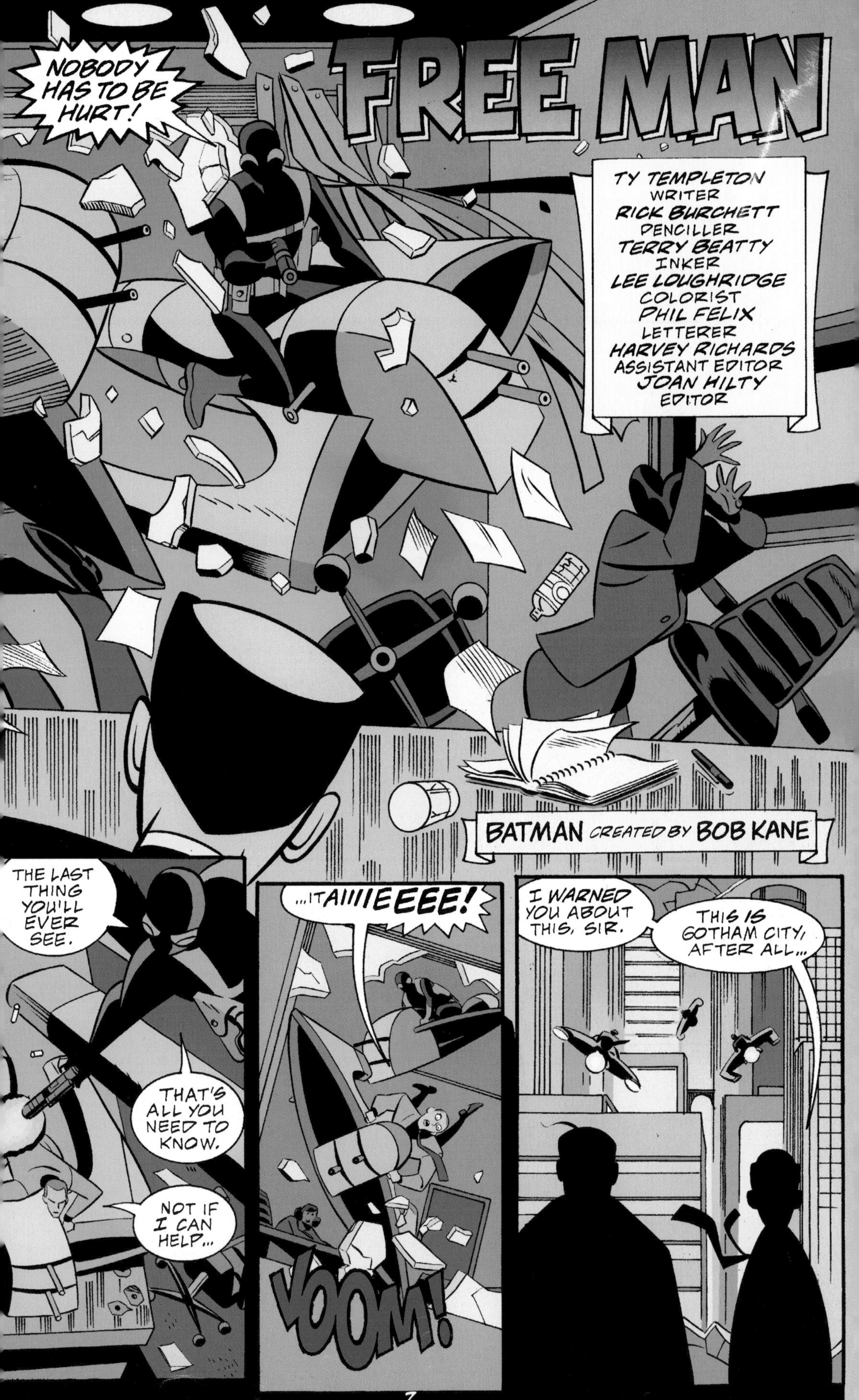

NOBODY HAS TO BE HURT!
FREE MAN
TY TEMPLETON WRITER
RICK BURCHETT PENCILLER
TERRY BEATTY INKER
LEE LOUGHRIDGE COLORIST
PHIL FELIX LETTERER
HARVEY RICHARDS ASSISTANT EDITOR
JOAN HILTY EDITOR
BATMAN CREATED BY BOB KANE
THE LAST THING YOU'LL EVER SEE.
THAT'S ALL YOU NEED TO KNOW.
NOT IF I CAN HELP...
...ITAIIIIEEEE!
VOOM!
I WARNED YOU ABOUT THIS, SIR.
THIS IS GOTHAM CITY, AFTER ALL...

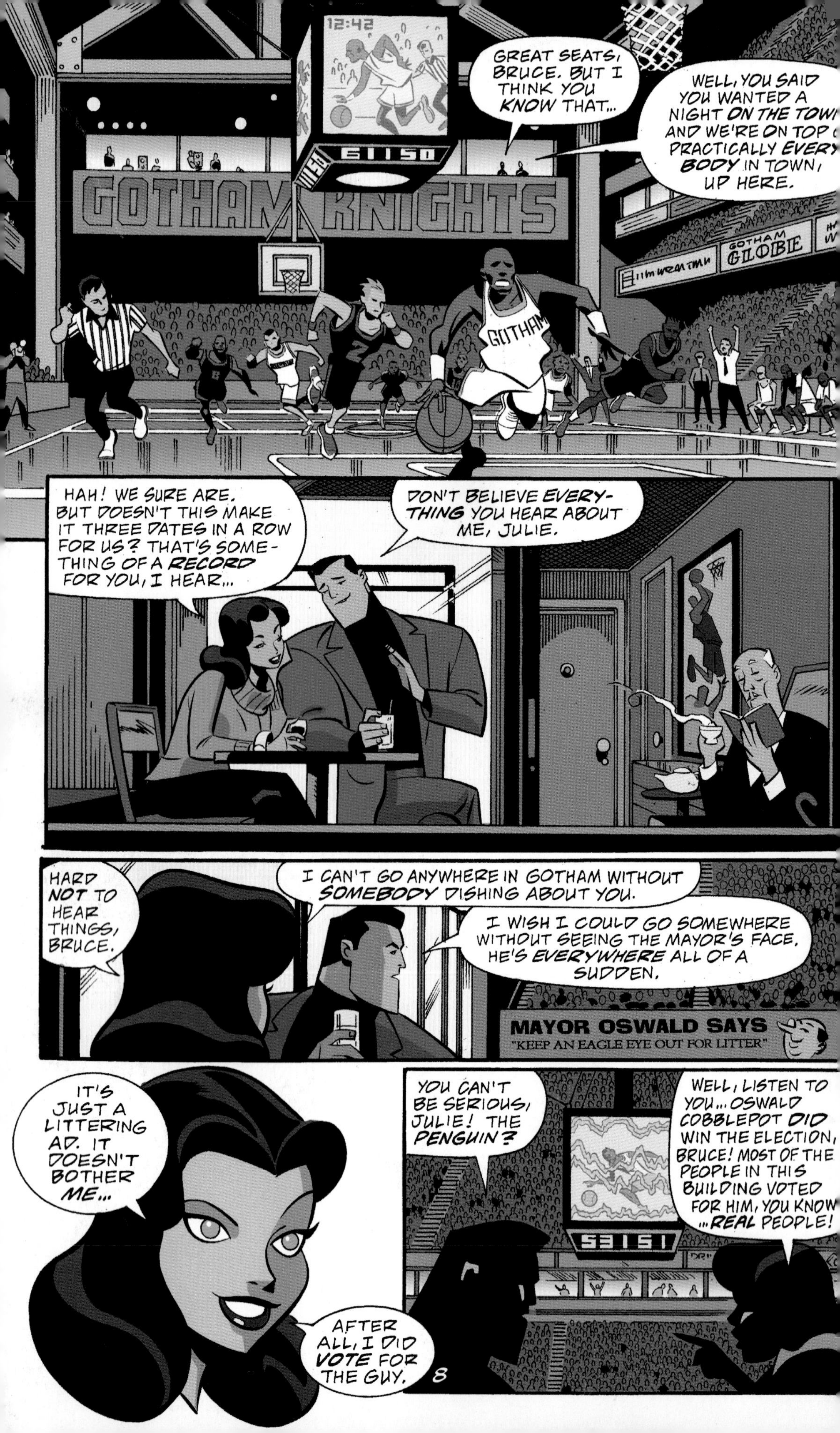
12:42
61 150
GOTHAM KNIGHTS
GOTHAM GLOBE
GOTHAM
GREAT SEATS, BRUCE. BUT I THINK YOU KNOW THAT...
WELL, YOU SAID YOU WANTED A NIGHT ON THE TOWN AND WE'RE ON TOP OF PRACTICALLY EVERYBODY IN TOWN, UP HERE.
HAH! WE SURE ARE. BUT DOESN'T THIS MAKE IT THREE DATES IN A ROW FOR US? THAT'S SOMETHING OF A RECORD FOR YOU, I HEAR...
DON'T BELIEVE EVERYTHING YOU HEAR ABOUT ME, JULIE.
HARD NOT TO HEAR THINGS, BRUCE.
I CAN'T GO ANYWHERE IN GOTHAM WITHOUT SOMEBODY DISHING ABOUT YOU.
I WISH I COULD GO SOMEWHERE WITHOUT SEEING THE MAYOR'S FACE. HE'S EVERYWHERE ALL OF A SUDDEN.
MAYOR OSWALD SAYS
"KEEP AN EAGLE EYE OUT FOR LITTER"
IT'S JUST A LITTERING AD. IT DOESN'T BOTHER ME...
AFTER ALL, I DID VOTE FOR THE GUY.
YOU CAN'T BE SERIOUS, JULIE! THE PENGUIN?
53 151
WELL, LISTEN TO YOU... OSWALD COBBLEPOT DID WIN THE ELECTION, BRUCE! MOST OF THE PEOPLE IN THIS BUILDING VOTED FOR HIM, YOU KNOW ...REAL PEOPLE!

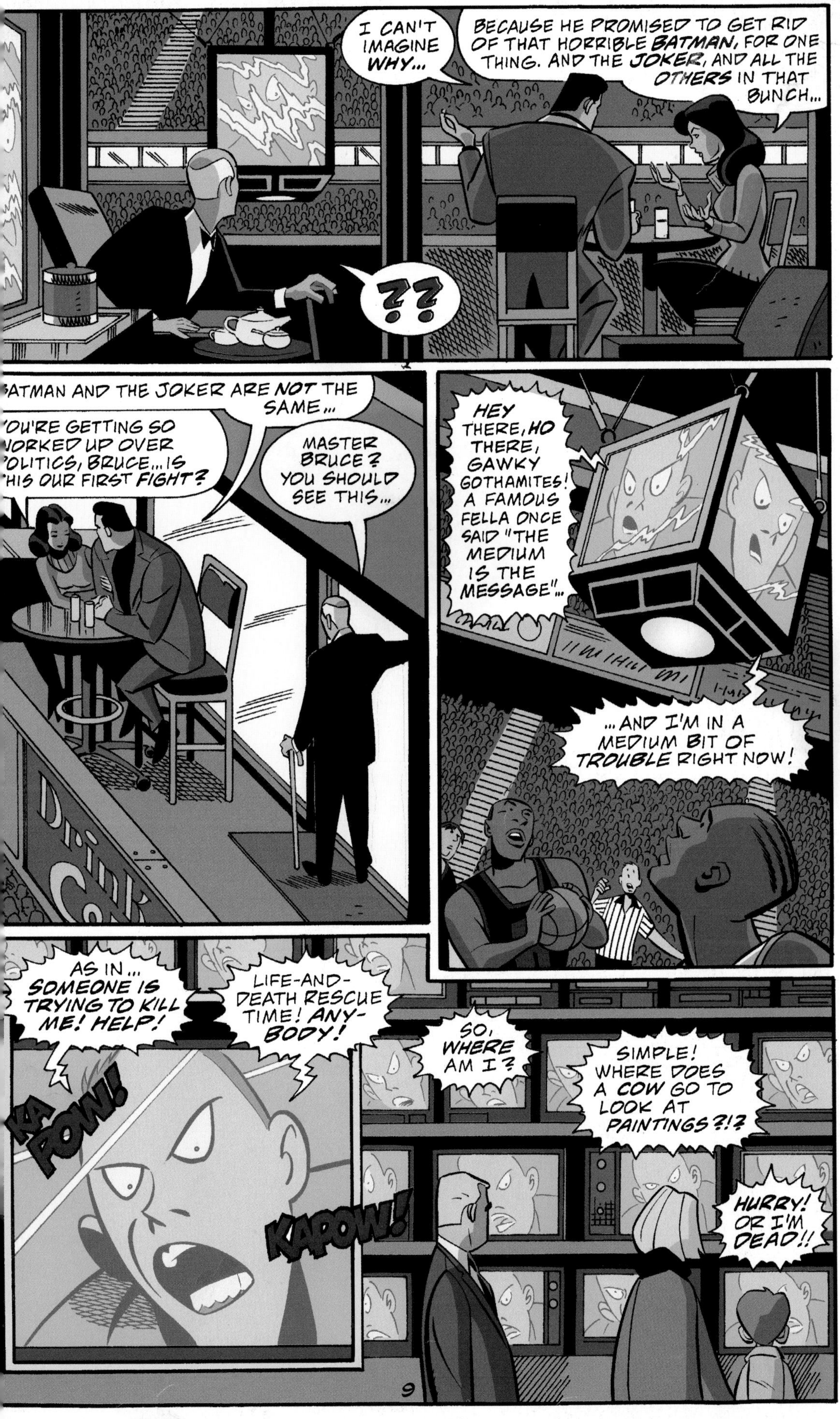

I CAN'T IMAGINE WHY...
BECAUSE HE PROMISED TO GET RID OF THAT HORRIBLE BATMAN, FOR ONE THING. AND THE JOKER, AND ALL THE OTHERS IN THAT BUNCH...
??
ATMAN AND THE JOKER ARE NOT THE SAME...
OU'RE GETTING SO ORKED UP OVER OLITICS, BRUCE... IS HIS OUR FIRST FIGHT?
MASTER BRUCE? YOU SHOULD SEE THIS...
HEY THERE, HO THERE, GAWKY GOTHAMITES! A FAMOUS FELLA ONCE SAID "THE MEDIUM IS THE MESSAGE"...
...AND I'M IN A MEDIUM BIT OF TROUBLE RIGHT NOW!
AS IN... SOMEONE IS TRYING TO KILL ME! HELP!
LIFE-AND-DEATH RESCUE TIME! ANYBODY!
KA POW!
KAPOW!
SO, WHERE AM I?
SIMPLE! WHERE DOES A COW GO TO LOOK AT PAINTINGS?!?
HURRY! OR I'M DEAD!!

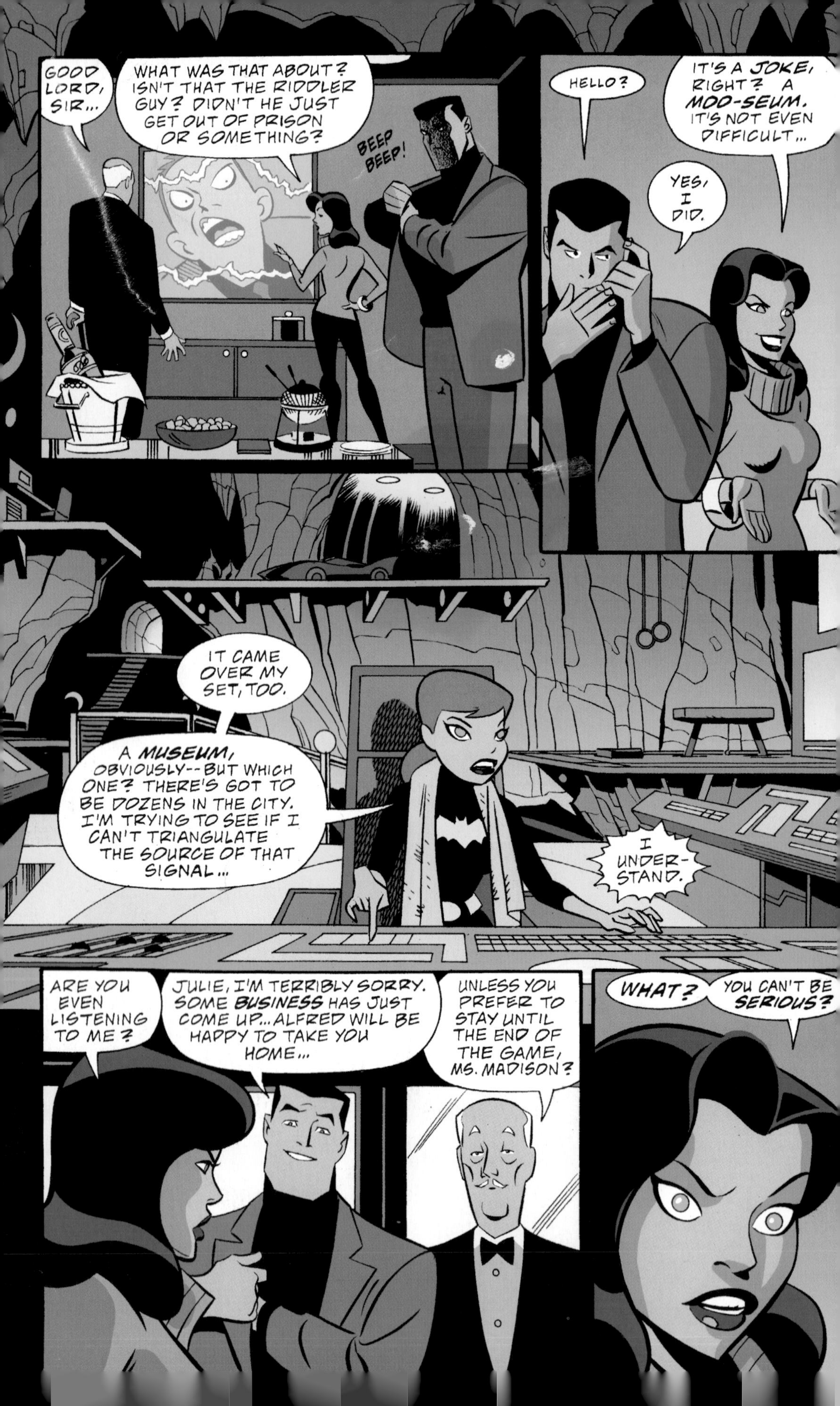

GOOD LORD, SIR...
WHAT WAS THAT ABOUT? ISN'T THAT THE RIDDLER GUY? DIDN'T HE JUST GET OUT OF PRISON OR SOMETHING?
BEEP BEEP!
HELLO?
IT'S A JOKE, RIGHT? A MOO-SEUM. IT'S NOT EVEN DIFFICULT...
YES, I DID.
IT CAME OVER MY SET, TOO.
A MUSEUM, OBVIOUSLY--BUT WHICH ONE? THERE'S GOT TO BE DOZENS IN THE CITY. I'M TRYING TO SEE IF I CAN'T TRIANGULATE THE SOURCE OF THAT SIGNAL...
I UNDER-STAND.
ARE YOU EVEN LISTENING TO ME?
JULIE, I'M TERRIBLY SORRY. SOME BUSINESS HAS JUST COME UP...ALFRED WILL BE HAPPY TO TAKE YOU HOME...
UNLESS YOU PREFER TO STAY UNTIL THE END OF THE GAME, MS. MADISON?
WHAT?
YOU CAN'T BE SERIOUS?

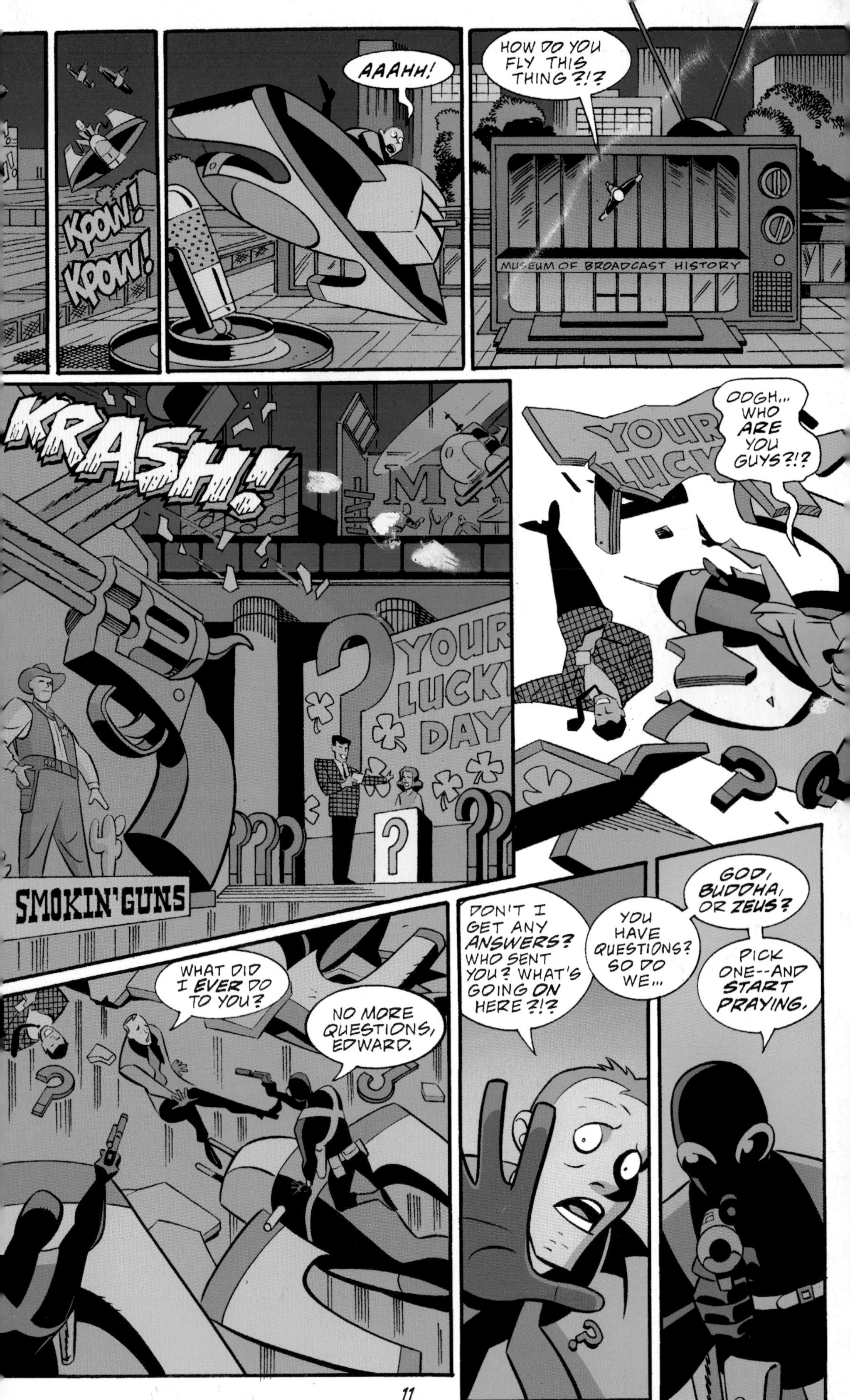
KPOW!
KPOW!
AAAHH!
HOW DO YOU FLY THIS THING?!?
MUSEUM OF BROADCAST HISTORY
KRASH!
YOUR LUCKY DAY
SMOKIN' GUNS
OOGH... WHO ARE YOU GUYS?!?
WHAT DID I EVER DO TO YOU?
NO MORE QUESTIONS, EDWARD.
DON'T I GET ANY ANSWERS? WHO SENT YOU? WHAT'S GOING ON HERE?!?
YOU HAVE QUESTIONS? SO DO WE...
GOD, BUDDHA, OR ZEUS?
PICK ONE--AND START PRAYING.

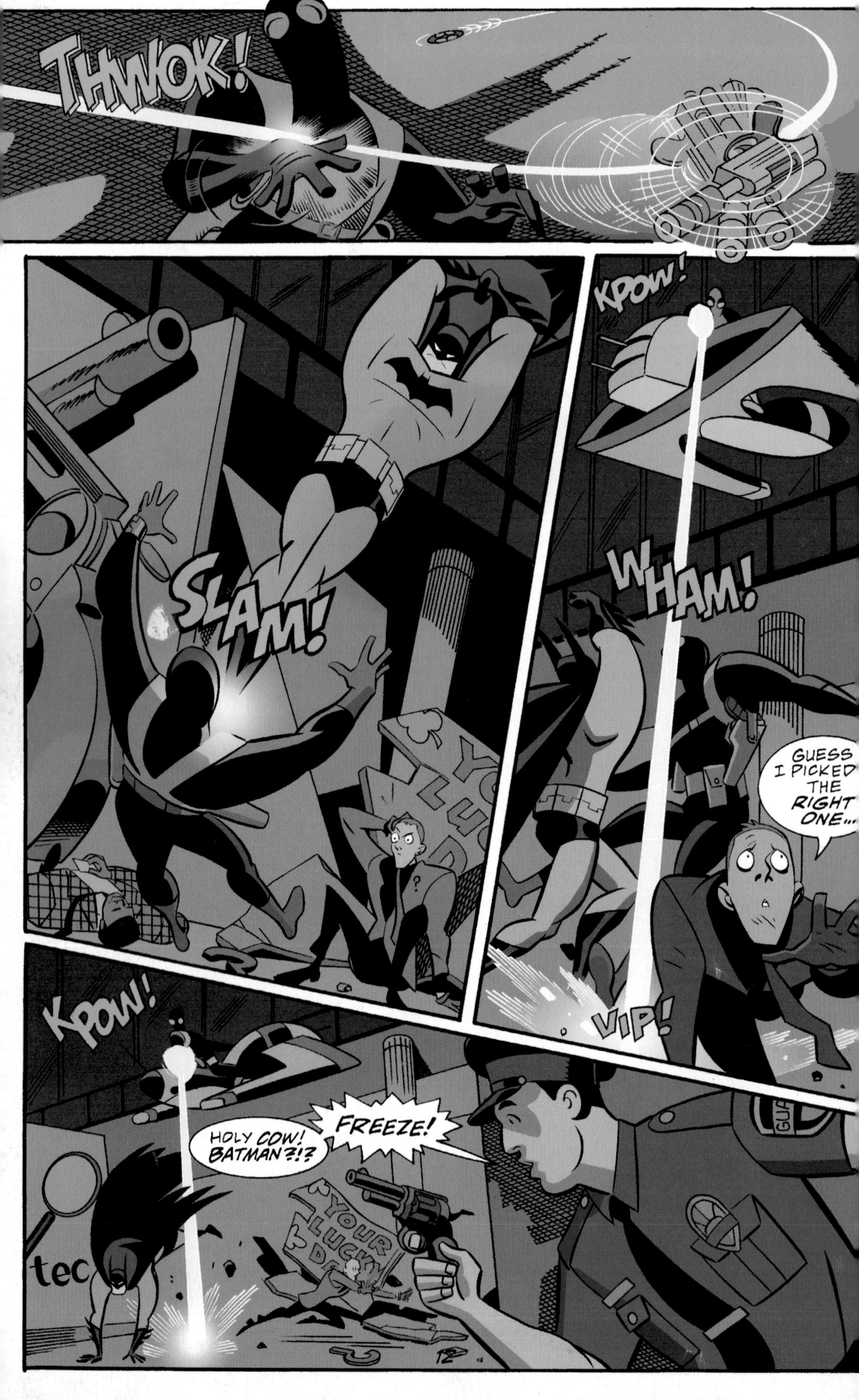
THWOK!
SLAM!
KPOW!
WHAM!
GUESS I PICKED THE RIGHT ONE...
VIP!
KPOW!
HOLY COW! BATMAN?!?
FREEZE!
YOUR LUCKY DAY
tec
12

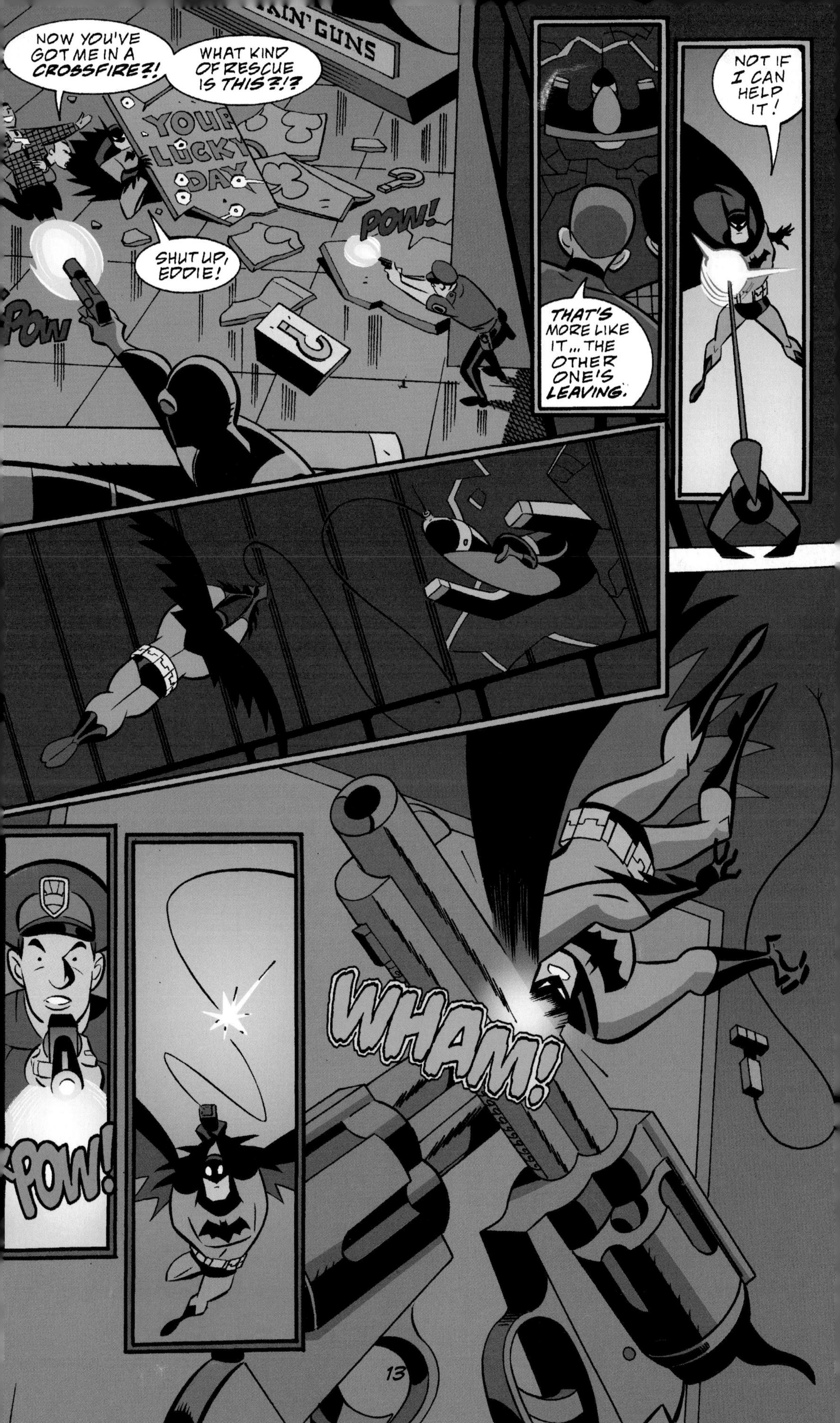
...KIN' GUNS
NOW YOU'VE GOT ME IN A CROSSFIRE?!
WHAT KIND OF RESCUE IS THIS?!?
YOUR LUCKY DAY
POW!
SHUT UP, EDDIE!
POW
THAT'S MORE LIKE IT... THE OTHER ONE'S LEAVING.
NOT IF I CAN HELP IT!
POW!
WHAM!

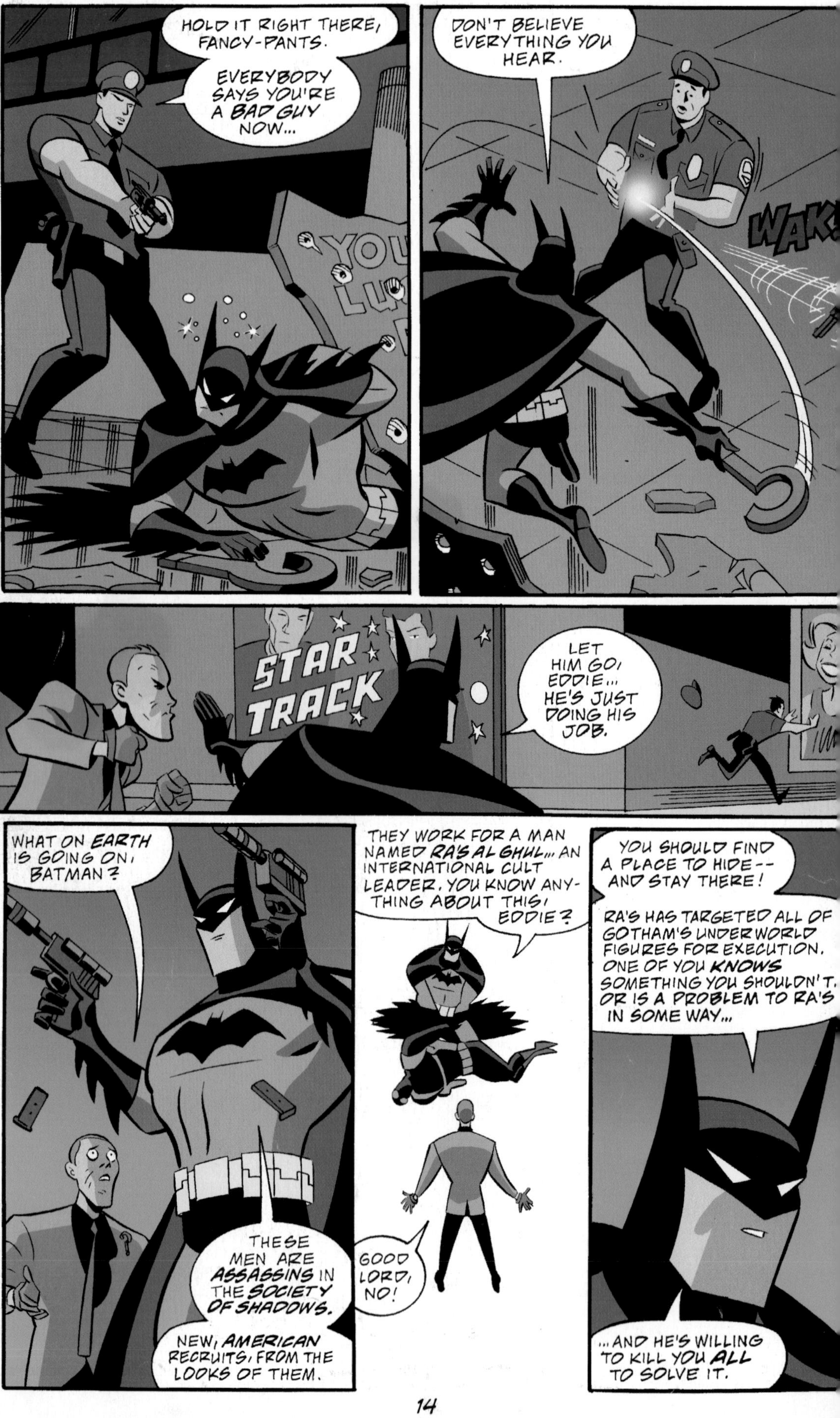
HOLD IT RIGHT THERE, FANCY-PANTS.
EVERYBODY SAYS YOU'RE A BAD GUY NOW...
YOU
DON'T BELIEVE EVERYTHING YOU HEAR.
WAK!
STAR TRACK
LET HIM GO, EDDIE... HE'S JUST DOING HIS JOB.
WHAT ON EARTH IS GOING ON, BATMAN?
THESE MEN ARE ASSASSINS IN THE SOCIETY OF SHADOWS.
NEW, AMERICAN RECRUITS, FROM THE LOOKS OF THEM.
THEY WORK FOR A MAN NAMED RA'S AL GHUL... AN INTERNATIONAL CULT LEADER. YOU KNOW ANYTHING ABOUT THIS, EDDIE?
GOOD LORD, NO!
YOU SHOULD FIND A PLACE TO HIDE-- AND STAY THERE!
RA'S HAS TARGETED ALL OF GOTHAM'S UNDERWORLD FIGURES FOR EXECUTION. ONE OF YOU KNOWS SOMETHING YOU SHOULDN'T. OR IS A PROBLEM TO RA'S IN SOME WAY...
...AND HE'S WILLING TO KILL YOU ALL TO SOLVE IT.

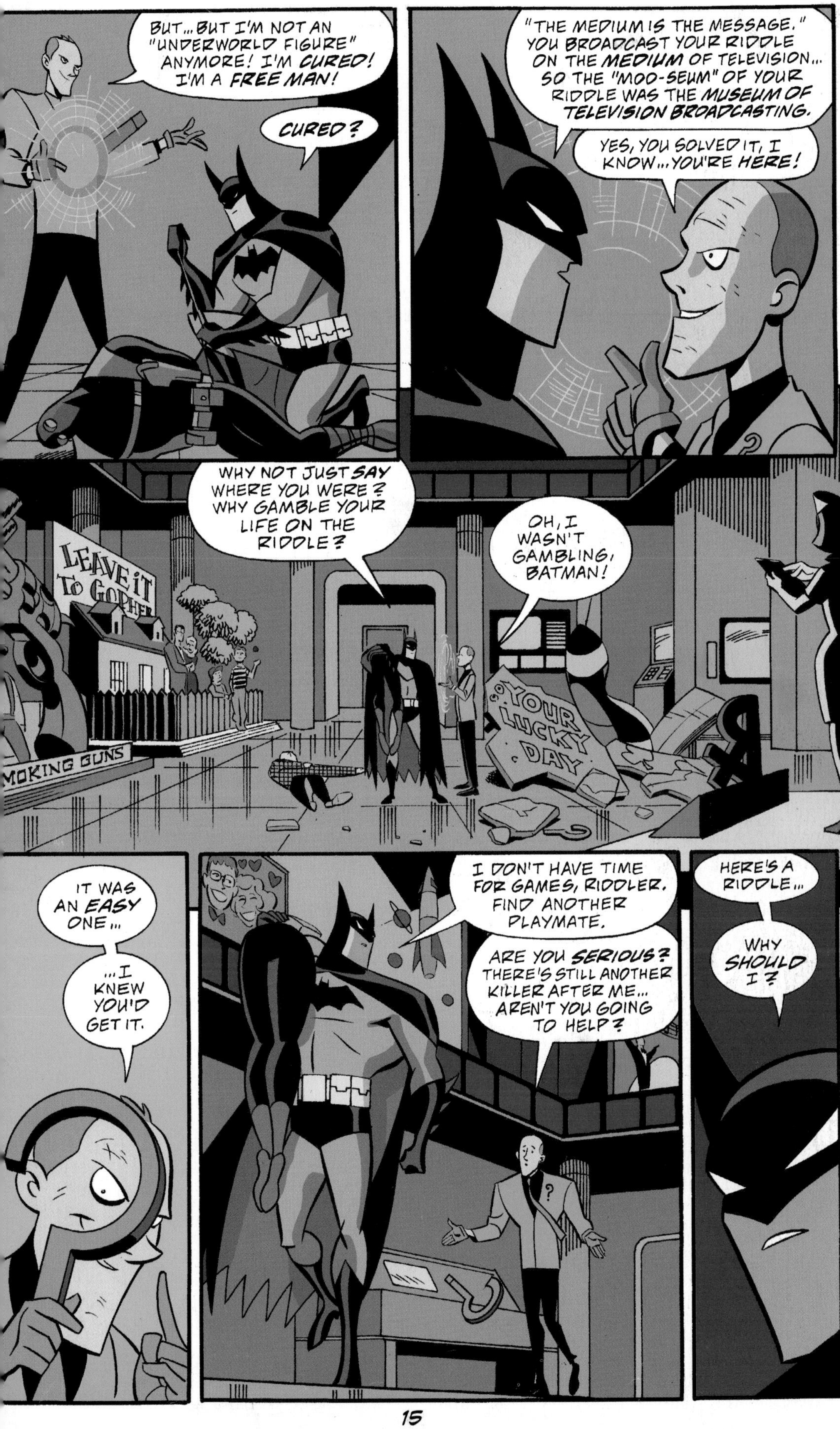

BUT... BUT I'M NOT AN "UNDERWORLD FIGURE" ANYMORE! I'M CURED! I'M A FREE MAN!
CURED?
"THE MEDIUM IS THE MESSAGE." YOU BROADCAST YOUR RIDDLE ON THE MEDIUM OF TELEVISION... SO THE "MOO-SEUM" OF YOUR RIDDLE WAS THE MUSEUM OF TELEVISION BROADCASTING.
YES, YOU SOLVED IT, I KNOW... YOU'RE HERE!
LEAVE IT TO GOPHER
MOKING GUNS
YOUR LUCKY DAY
WHY NOT JUST SAY WHERE YOU WERE? WHY GAMBLE YOUR LIFE ON THE RIDDLE?
OH, I WASN'T GAMBLING, BATMAN!
IT WAS AN EASY ONE...
...I KNEW YOU'D GET IT.
I DON'T HAVE TIME FOR GAMES, RIDDLER. FIND ANOTHER PLAYMATE.
ARE YOU SERIOUS? THERE'S STILL ANOTHER KILLER AFTER ME... AREN'T YOU GOING TO HELP?
HERE'S A RIDDLE...
WHY SHOULD I?

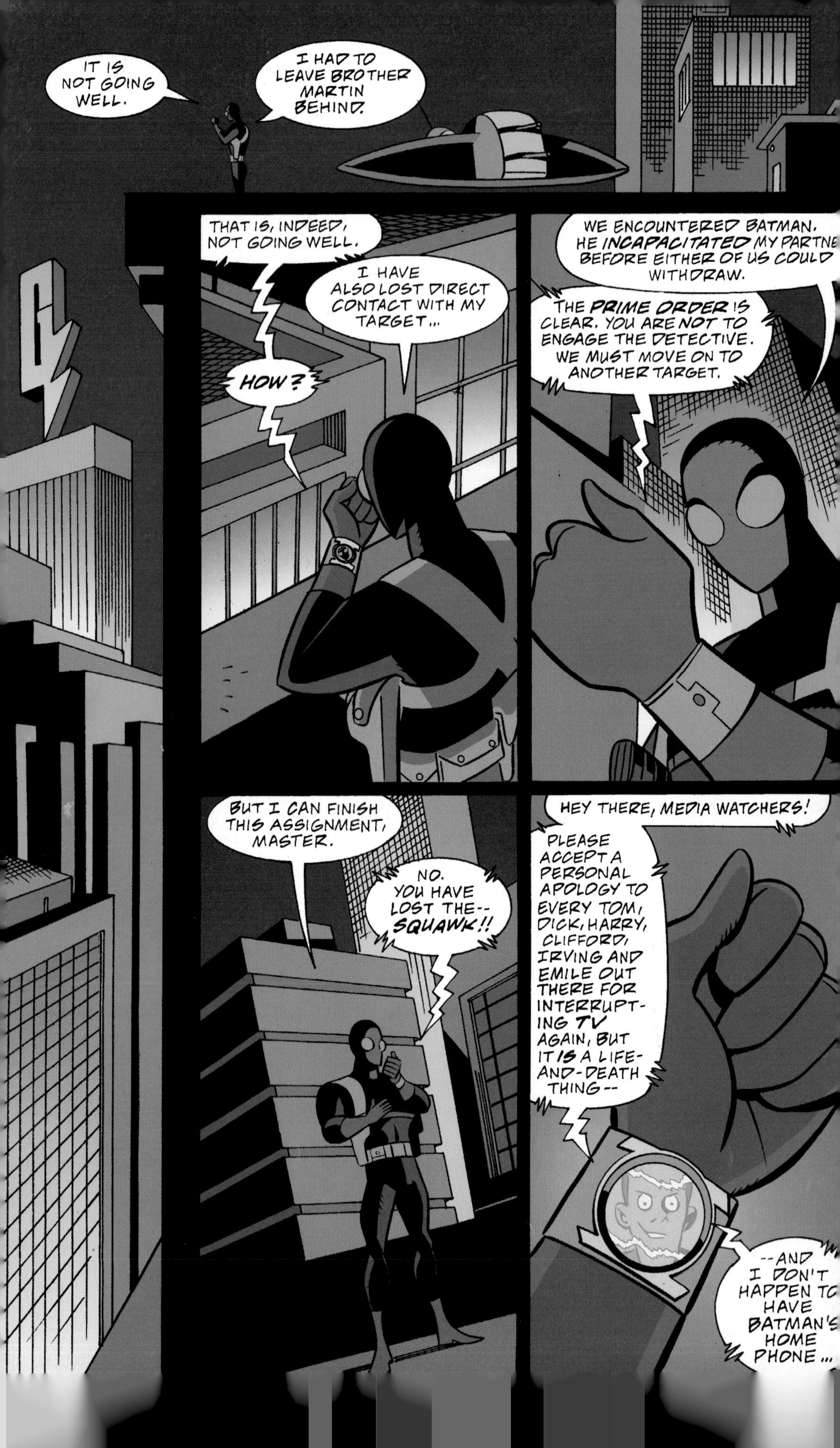
IT IS NOT GOING WELL.
I HAD TO LEAVE BROTHER MARTIN BEHIND.
THAT IS, INDEED, NOT GOING WELL.
I HAVE ALSO LOST DIRECT CONTACT WITH MY TARGET...
HOW?
WE ENCOUNTERED BATMAN. HE INCAPACITATED MY PARTNE BEFORE EITHER OF US COULD WITHDRAW.
THE PRIME ORDER IS CLEAR. YOU ARE NOT TO ENGAGE THE DETECTIVE. WE MUST MOVE ON TO ANOTHER TARGET.
BUT I CAN FINISH THIS ASSIGNMENT, MASTER.
NO. YOU HAVE LOST THE-- SQUAWK!!
HEY THERE, MEDIA WATCHERS!
PLEASE ACCEPT A PERSONAL APOLOGY TO EVERY TOM, DICK, HARRY, CLIFFORD, IRVING AND EMILE OUT THERE FOR INTERRUPT-ING TV AGAIN, BUT IT IS A LIFE-AND-DEATH THING--
--AND I DON'T HAPPEN TO HAVE BATMAN'S HOME PHONE...

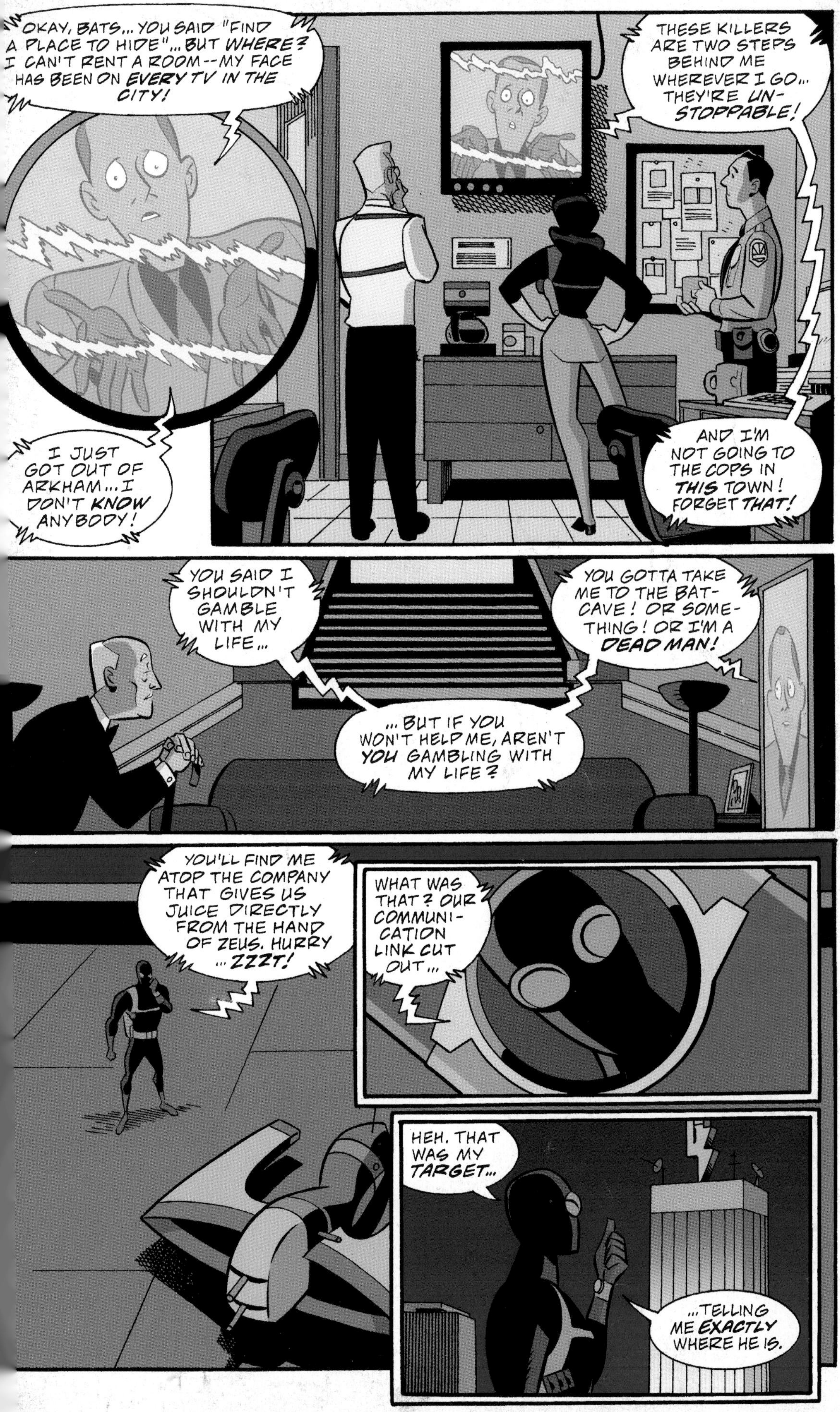
OKAY, BATS... YOU SAID "FIND A PLACE TO HIDE"... BUT WHERE? I CAN'T RENT A ROOM--MY FACE HAS BEEN ON EVERY TV IN THE CITY!
I JUST GOT OUT OF ARKHAM... I DON'T KNOW ANYBODY!
THESE KILLERS ARE TWO STEPS BEHIND ME WHEREVER I GO... THEY'RE UN-STOPPABLE!
AND I'M NOT GOING TO THE COPS IN THIS TOWN! FORGET THAT!
YOU SAID I SHOULDN'T GAMBLE WITH MY LIFE...
YOU GOTTA TAKE ME TO THE BAT-CAVE! OR SOME-THING! OR I'M A DEAD MAN!
...BUT IF YOU WON'T HELP ME, AREN'T YOU GAMBLING WITH MY LIFE?
YOU'LL FIND ME ATOP THE COMPANY THAT GIVES US JUICE DIRECTLY FROM THE HAND OF ZEUS. HURRY ...ZZZT!
WHAT WAS THAT? OUR COMMUNI-CATION LINK CUT OUT...
HEH. THAT WAS MY TARGET...
...TELLING ME EXACTLY WHERE HE IS.

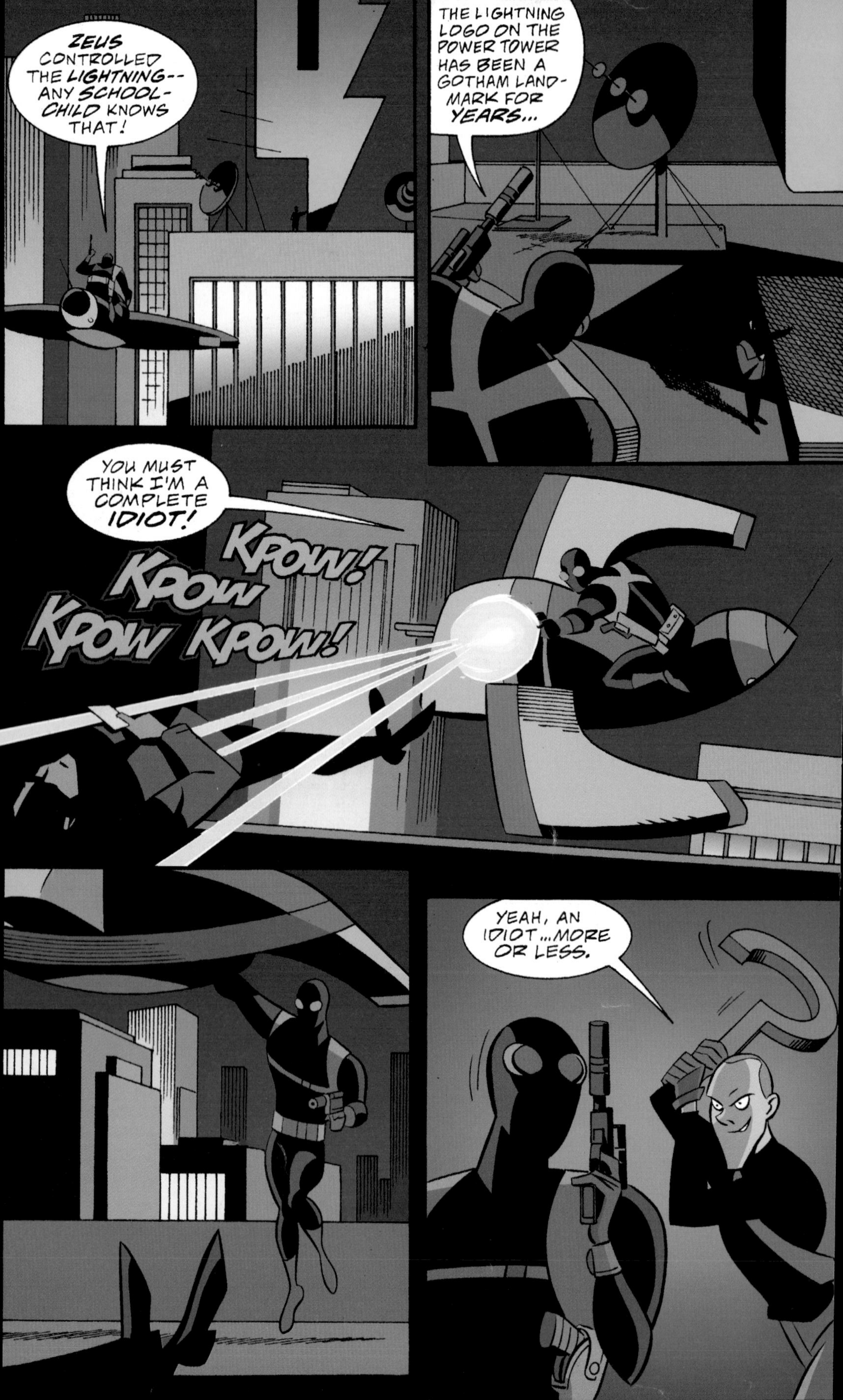
ZEUS CONTROLLED THE LIGHTNING-- ANY SCHOOL-CHILD KNOWS THAT!
THE LIGHTNING LOGO ON THE POWER TOWER HAS BEEN A GOTHAM LAND-MARK FOR YEARS...
YOU MUST THINK I'M A COMPLETE IDIOT!
KPOW! KPOW KPOW KPOW!
YEAH, AN IDIOT...MORE OR LESS.

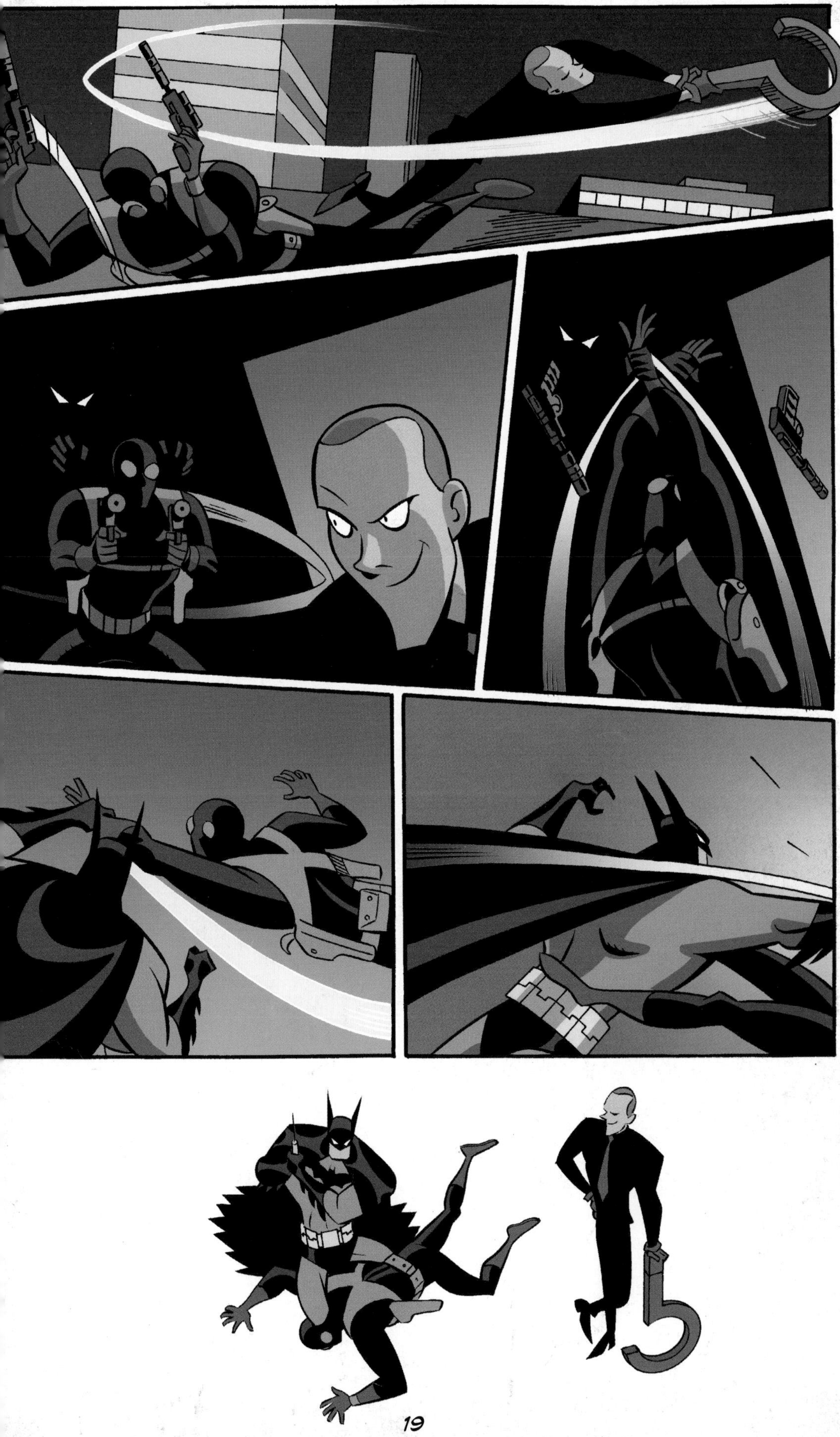

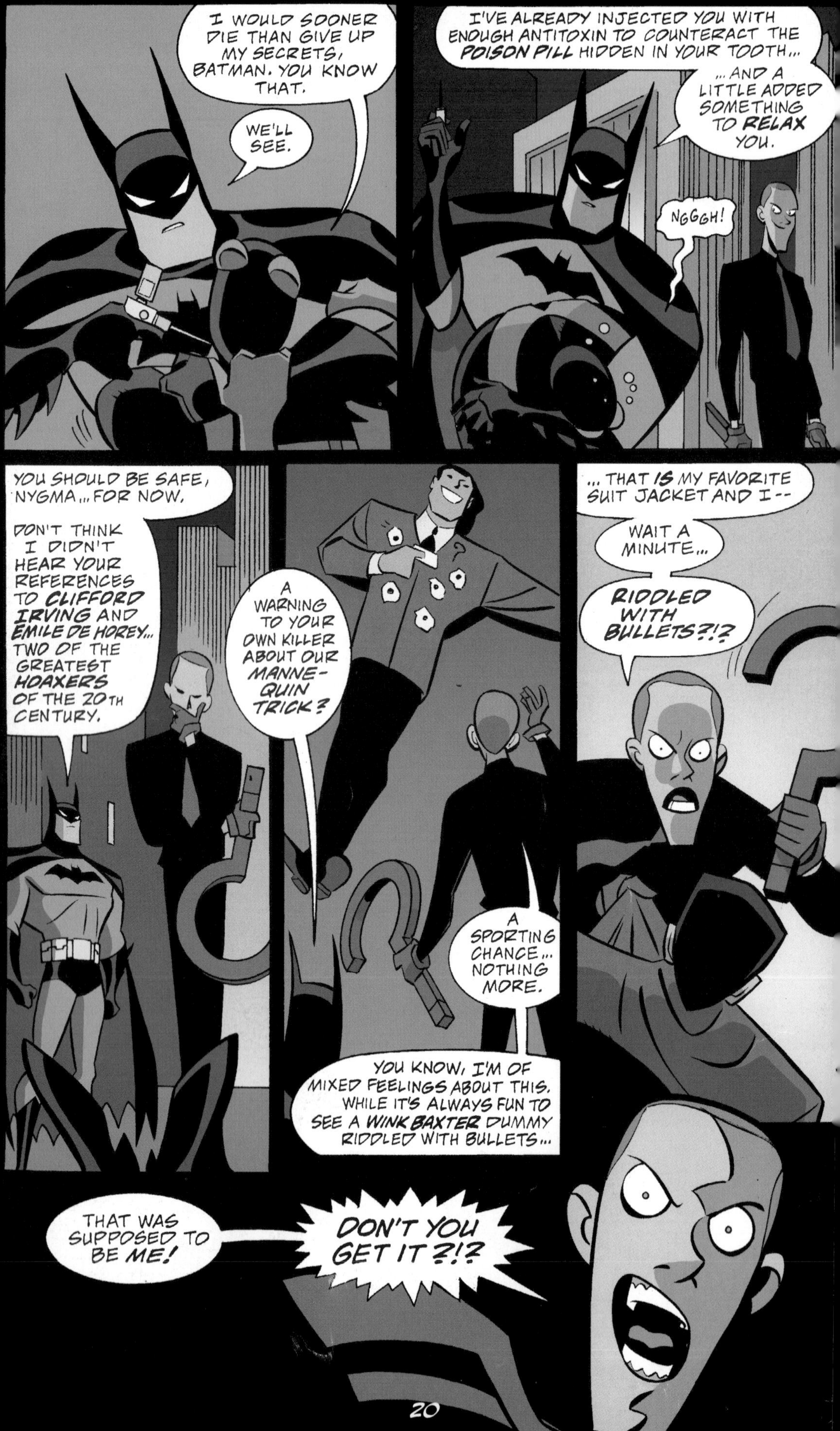

I WOULD SOONER DIE THAN GIVE UP MY SECRETS, BATMAN. YOU KNOW THAT.
WE'LL SEE.
I'VE ALREADY INJECTED YOU WITH ENOUGH ANTITOXIN TO COUNTERACT THE POISON PILL HIDDEN IN YOUR TOOTH...
...AND A LITTLE ADDED SOMETHING TO RELAX YOU.
NGGGH!
YOU SHOULD BE SAFE, NYGMA...FOR NOW.
DON'T THINK I DIDN'T HEAR YOUR REFERENCES TO CLIFFORD IRVING AND EMILE DE HOREY... TWO OF THE GREATEST HOAXERS OF THE 20TH CENTURY.
A WARNING TO YOUR OWN KILLER ABOUT OUR MANNEQUIN TRICK?
A SPORTING CHANCE... NOTHING MORE.
YOU KNOW, I'M OF MIXED FEELINGS ABOUT THIS. WHILE IT'S ALWAYS FUN TO SEE A WINK BAXTER DUMMY RIDDLED WITH BULLETS...
...THAT IS MY FAVORITE SUIT JACKET AND I--
WAIT A MINUTE...
RIDDLED WITH BULLETS?!?
THAT WAS SUPPOSED TO BE ME!
DON'T YOU GET IT?!?

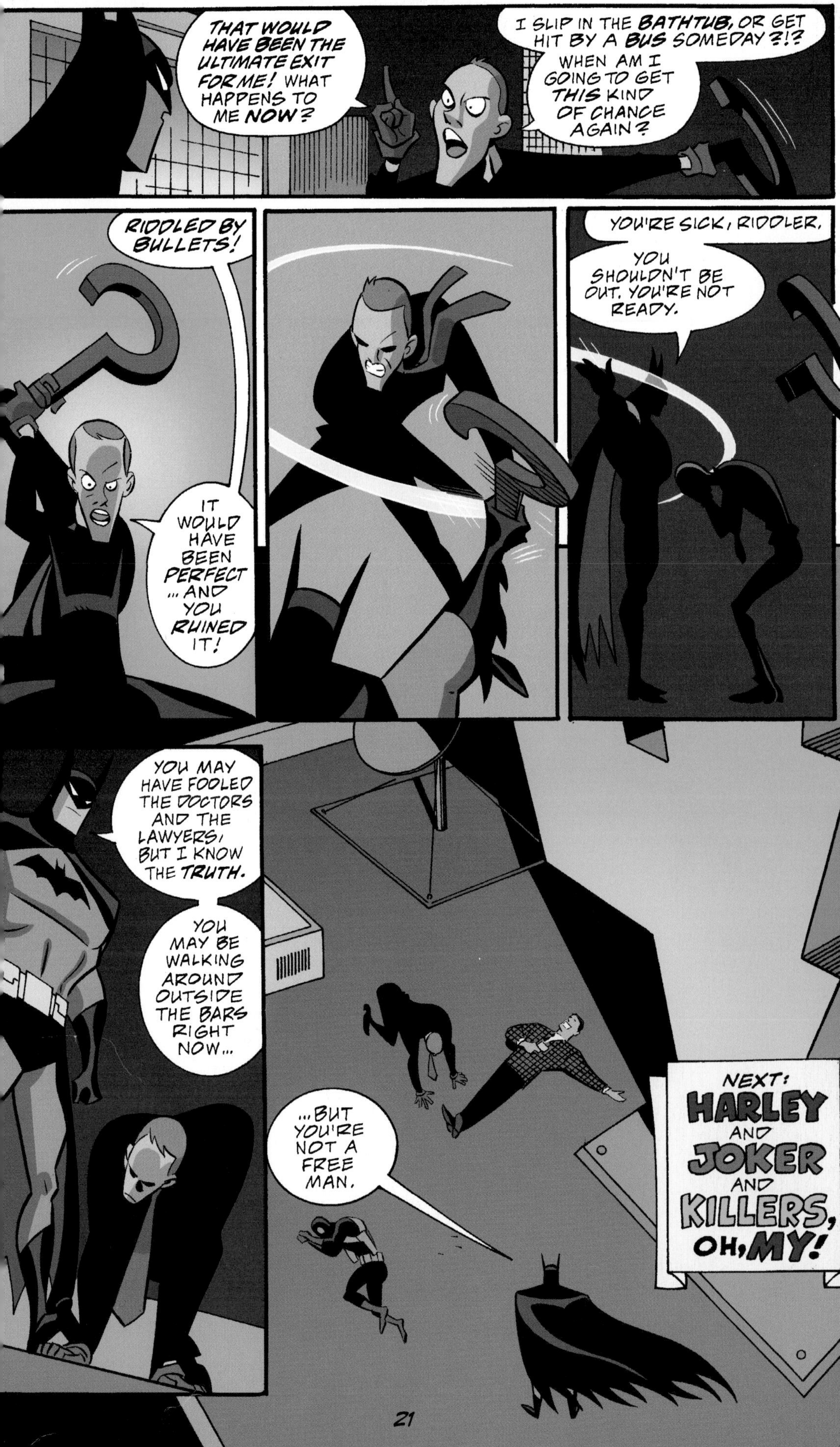

THAT WOULD HAVE BEEN THE ULTIMATE EXIT FOR ME! WHAT HAPPENS TO ME NOW?
I SLIP IN THE BATHTUB, OR GET HIT BY A BUS SOMEDAY?!?
WHEN AM I GOING TO GET THIS KIND OF CHANCE AGAIN?
RIDDLED BY BULLETS!
IT WOULD HAVE BEEN PERFECT ...AND YOU RUINED IT!
YOU'RE SICK, RIDDLER.
YOU SHOULDN'T BE OUT. YOU'RE NOT READY.
YOU MAY HAVE FOOLED THE DOCTORS AND THE LAWYERS, BUT I KNOW THE TRUTH.
YOU MAY BE WALKING AROUND OUTSIDE THE BARS RIGHT NOW...
...BUT YOU'RE NOT A FREE MAN.
NEXT: HARLEY AND JOKER AND KILLERS, OH, MY!

WAUGH-WA-WA.

IT SEEMS ONLY FITTING THAT A *GROUND-BREAKING* MAYOR LIKE *MYSELF*...

...IS BREAKING *GROUND* AT THE SITE OF THIS NEW VENTURE!

future site of MAMMOTH STUDIOS

GRAY GHOST

AC CONS

THANKS TO MY TIRELESS EFFORTS, *MAMMOTH STUDIOS* WILL BE SETTING UP SHOP IN OUR FAIR CITY!

SOME POLITICOS MAY *PROMISE* YOU THE STARS, BUT OSWALD C. COBBLEPOT *DELIVERS!*

GOTHAM CITY WELCOMES THE future site of MAMMOTH STUDIOS

MY DEAR CONSTITUENTS...

...THIS WON'T JUST BRING BUSINESS AND TOURISM TO GOTHAM. IT WILL *ALSO* BRING...

...A TOUCH OF *CLASS!*

CLAP CLAP CLAP CLAP CLAP CLAP!

SLOTT--WRITER
TEMPLETON--PENCILLER
BEATTY--INKER
ZYLONOL--COLORIST
FELIX--LETTERER
RICHARDS--ASSISTANT
HILTY--EDITOR
BATMAN CREATED BY *BOB KANE*

FOWL PLAY

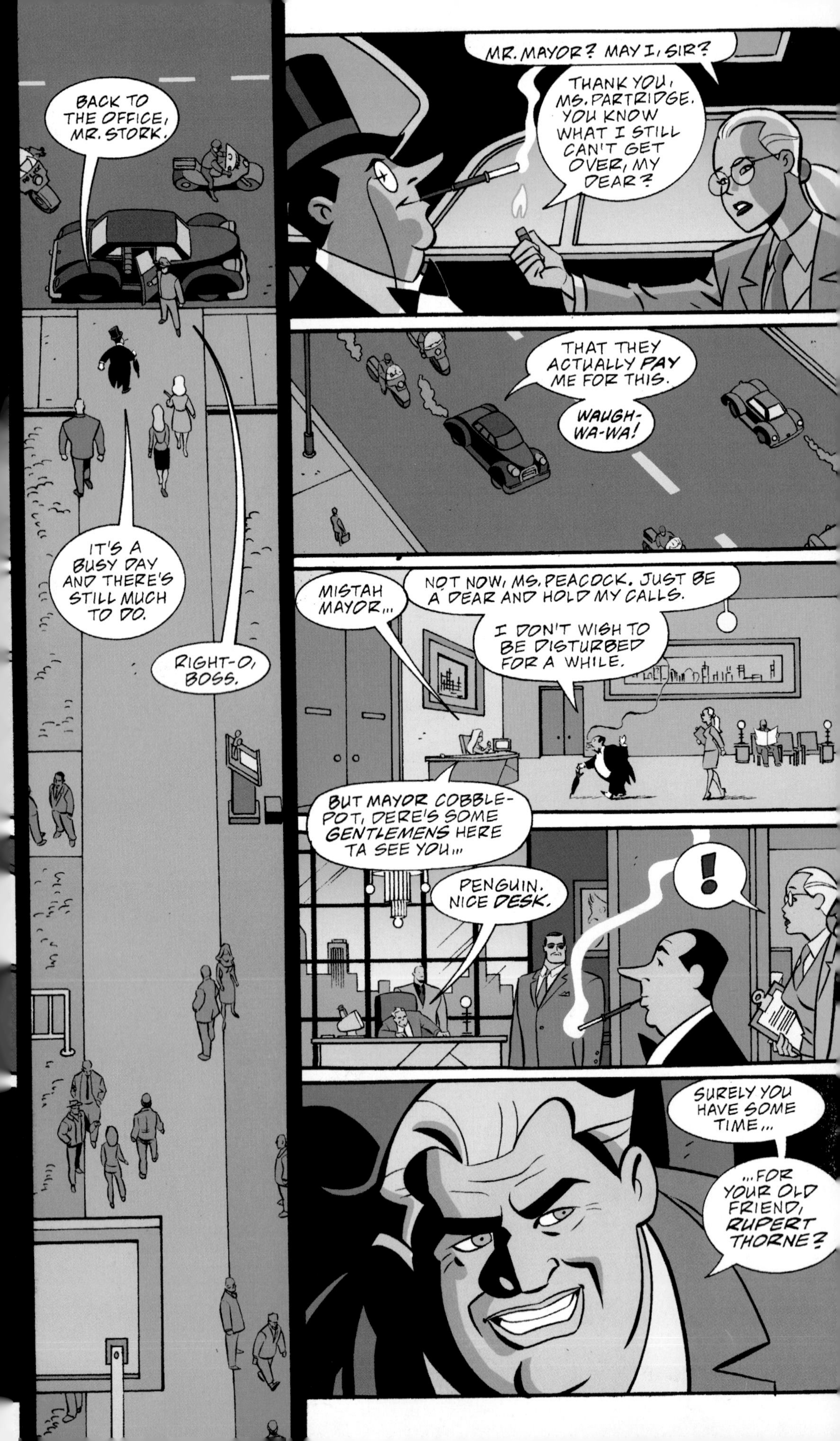

BACK TO THE OFFICE, MR. STORK.
IT'S A BUSY DAY AND THERE'S STILL MUCH TO DO.
RIGHT-O, BOSS.
MR. MAYOR? MAY I, SIR?
THANK YOU, MS. PARTRIDGE. YOU KNOW WHAT I STILL CAN'T GET OVER, MY DEAR?
THAT THEY ACTUALLY PAY ME FOR THIS.
WAUGH-WA-WA!
MISTAH MAYOR...
NOT NOW, MS. PEACOCK. JUST BE A DEAR AND HOLD MY CALLS.
I DON'T WISH TO BE DISTURBED FOR A WHILE.
BUT MAYOR COBBLEPOT, DERE'S SOME GENTLEMENS HERE TA SEE YOU...
PENGUIN. NICE DESK.
!
SURELY YOU HAVE SOME TIME...
...FOR YOUR OLD FRIEND, RUPERT THORNE?

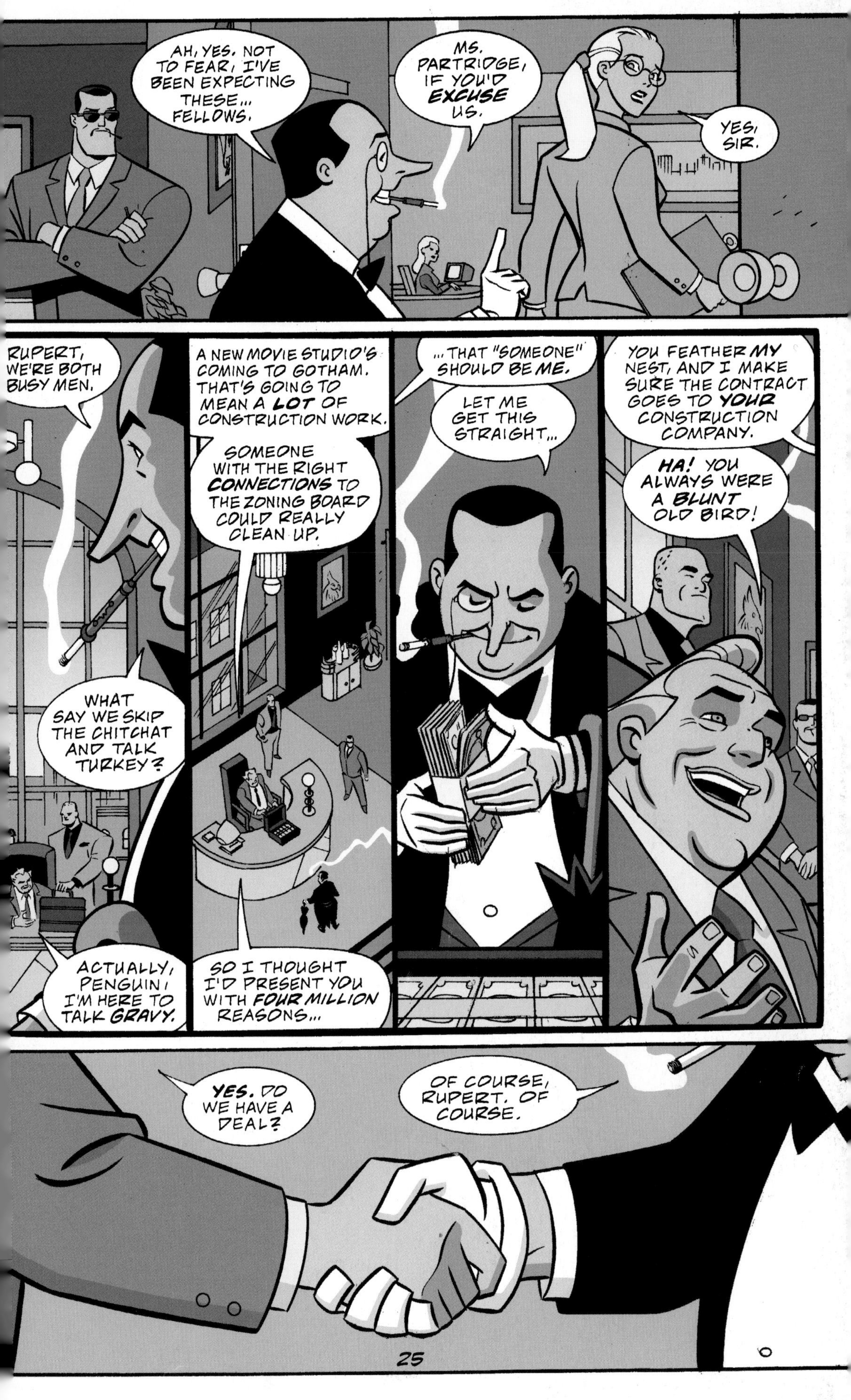
AH, YES. NOT TO FEAR, I'VE BEEN EXPECTING THESE... FELLOWS.
MS. PARTRIDGE, IF YOU'D EXCUSE US.
YES, SIR.
RUPERT, WE'RE BOTH BUSY MEN.
WHAT SAY WE SKIP THE CHITCHAT AND TALK TURKEY?
ACTUALLY, PENGUIN, I'M HERE TO TALK GRAVY.
A NEW MOVIE STUDIO'S COMING TO GOTHAM. THAT'S GOING TO MEAN A LOT OF CONSTRUCTION WORK.
SOMEONE WITH THE RIGHT CONNECTIONS TO THE ZONING BOARD COULD REALLY CLEAN UP.
SO I THOUGHT I'D PRESENT YOU WITH FOUR MILLION REASONS...
...THAT "SOMEONE" SHOULD BE ME.
LET ME GET THIS STRAIGHT...
YOU FEATHER MY NEST, AND I MAKE SURE THE CONTRACT GOES TO YOUR CONSTRUCTION COMPANY.
HA! YOU ALWAYS WERE A BLUNT OLD BIRD!
YES. DO WE HAVE A DEAL?
OF COURSE, RUPERT. OF COURSE.

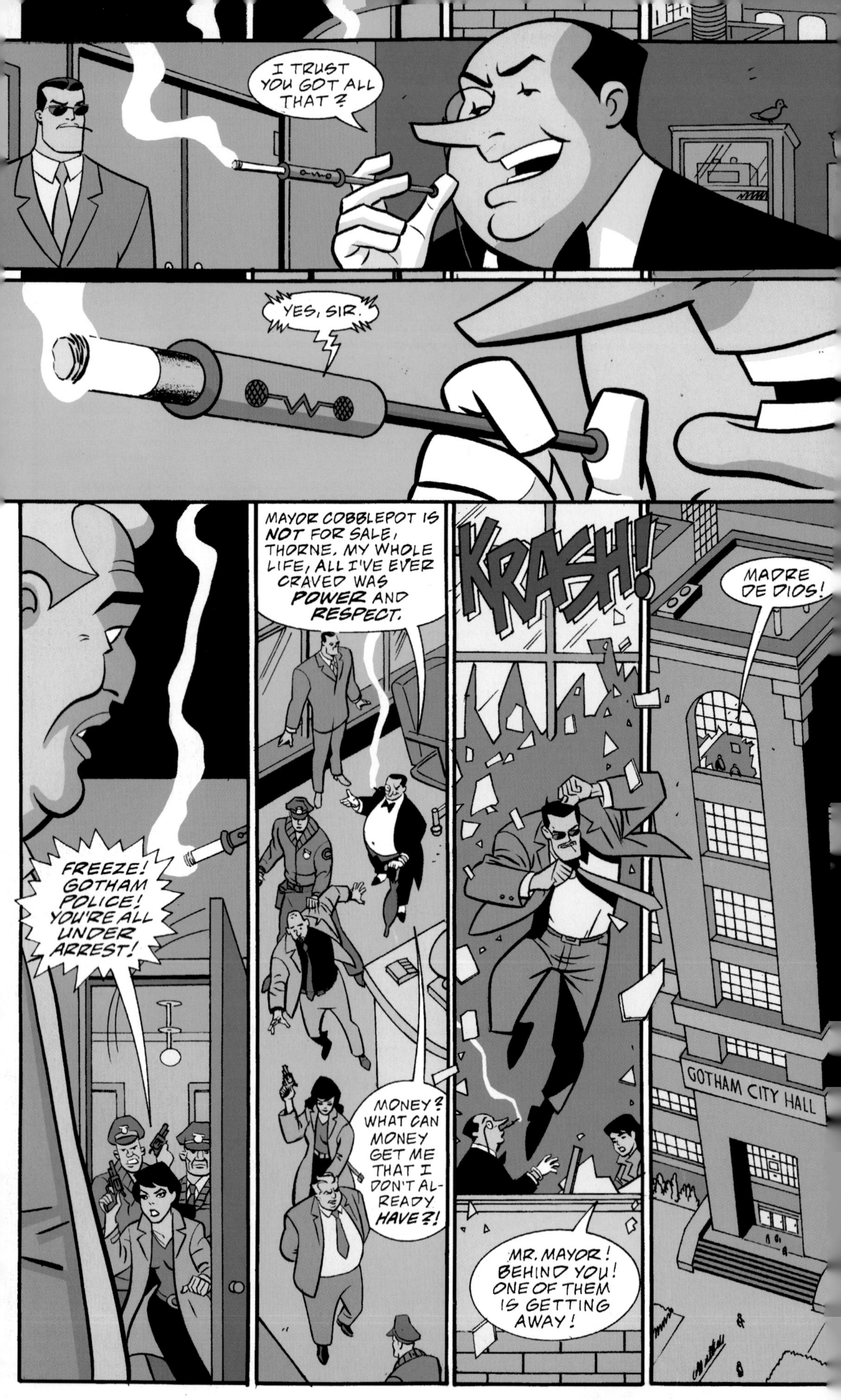

I TRUST YOU GOT ALL THAT?
YES, SIR.
FREEZE! GOTHAM POLICE! YOU'RE ALL UNDER ARREST!
MAYOR COBBLEPOT IS **NOT** FOR SALE, THORNE. MY WHOLE LIFE, ALL I'VE EVER CRAVED WAS **POWER** AND **RESPECT**.
MONEY? WHAT CAN MONEY GET ME THAT I DON'T AL-READY **HAVE**?!
KRASH!
MR. MAYOR! BEHIND YOU! ONE OF THEM IS GETTING AWAY!
MADRE DE DIOS!
GOTHAM CITY HALL

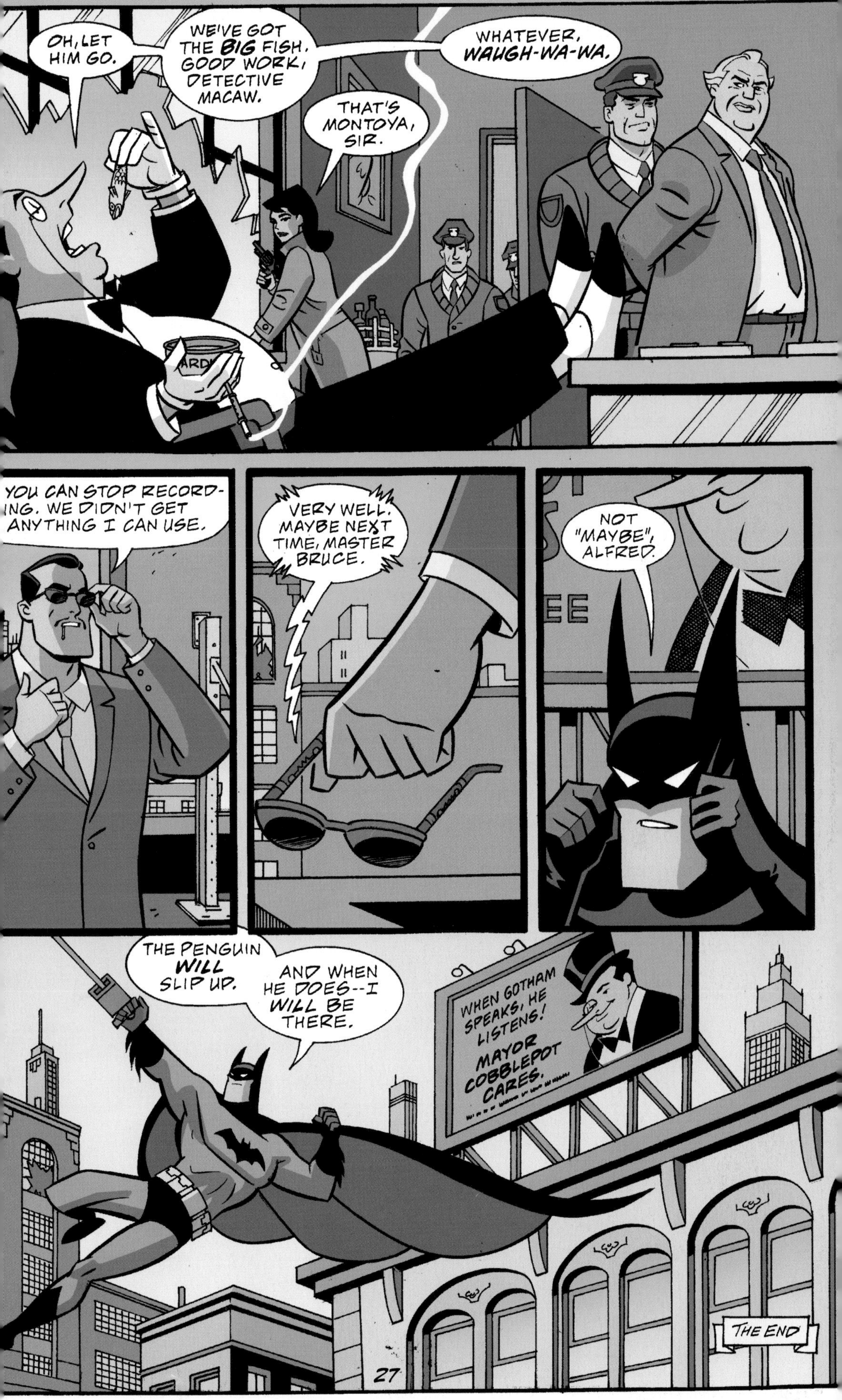
OH, LET HIM GO.
WE'VE GOT THE BIG FISH. GOOD WORK, DETECTIVE MACAW.
THAT'S MONTOYA, SIR.
WHATEVER. WAUGH-WA-WA.
YOU CAN STOP RECORDING. WE DIDN'T GET ANYTHING I CAN USE.
VERY WELL. MAYBE NEXT TIME, MASTER BRUCE.
NOT "MAYBE", ALFRED.
THE PENGUIN WILL SLIP UP.
AND WHEN HE DOES--I WILL BE THERE.
WHEN GOTHAM SPEAKS, HE LISTENS! MAYOR COBBLEPOT CARES.
THE END

CREATORS

TY TEMPLETON **WRITER & PENCILLER**

Ty Templeton was born in the wilds of downtown Toronto, Canada to a show-business family. He makes his living writing and drawing comic books, working on such characters as Batman, Superman, Spider-Man, The Simpsons, the Avengers, and many others.

DAN SLOTT **WRITER**

Dan Slott is a comics writer best known for his work on DC Comics' *Arkham Asylum*, and, for Marvel, *The Avengers* and the *Amazing Spider-Man*.

RICK BURCHETT **PENCILLER**

Rick Burchett has worked as a comics artist for more than 25 years. He has received the comics industry's Eisner Award three times, Spain's Haxtur Award, and he has been nominated for England's Eagle Award. Rick lives with his wife and two sons near St. Louis, Missouri.

TERRY BEATTY **INKER**

For more than ten years, Terry Beatty was the main inker of DC Comics' "animated-style" Batman comics, including *The Batman Strikes*. More recently, he worked on *Return to Perdition*, a graphic novel for DC's Vertigo Crime.

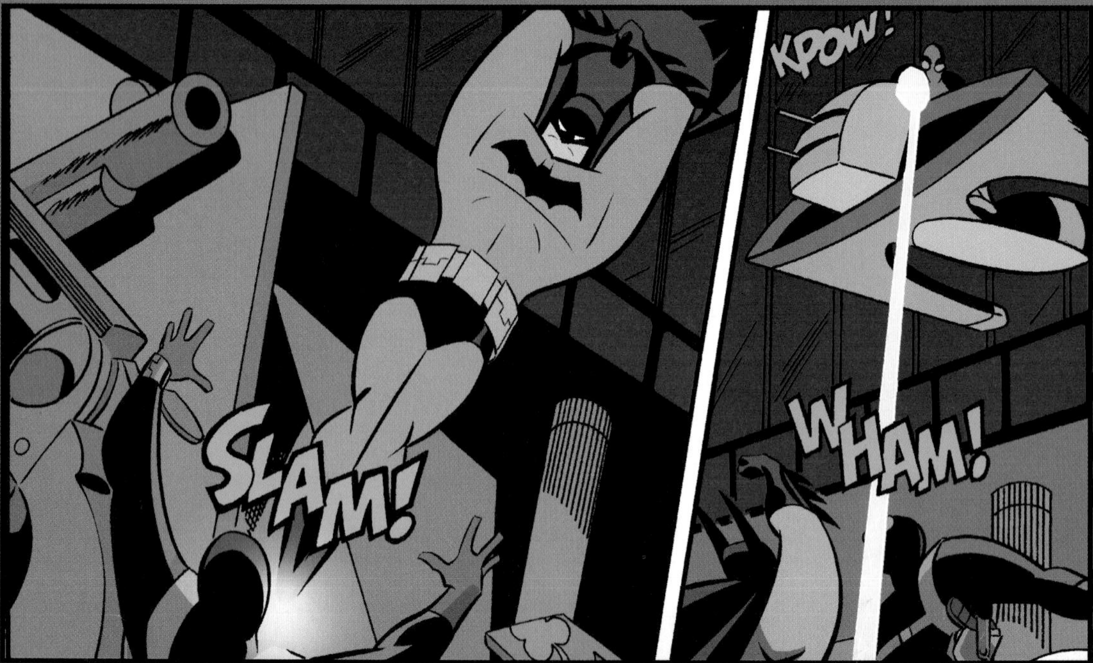
KPOW!
SLAM!
WHAM!

GLOSSARY

antitoxin (ant-ee-TOK-sin)--an antibody that is formed in response to an usually poisonous substance introduced into the body

assassin (uh-SASS-uhn)--a person who kills another person, often for money

cult (KUHLT)--a group of persons who belong to or show devotion to a person, idea, or thing

execution (ek-suh-KYOO-shuhn)--the act or process of putting someone to death

incapacitated (in-kuh-PASS-uh-tay-tuhd)--disabled or to make incapable

objection (ob-JEKT-shuhn)--a reason for or a feeling of disapproval

politics (POL-uh-tiks)--the art of guiding or influencing governmental policy

recruit (ri-KROOT)--newcomer to a field or activity

society (suh-SYE-uh-tee)--the community life thought of as a system within which the individuals live

underworld (UHN-dur-wurld)--the world of organized crime

venture (VEN-chur)--to go ahead in spite of danger

zoning (ZOH-ning)--divided (as a city) into sections for different purposes

BATMAN GLOSSARY

Alfred Pennyworth: Bruce Wayne's loyal butler. He knows Bruce Wayne's secret identity and helps the Dark Knight solve crimes in Gotham City.

Bruce Wayne: orphaned as a child, this wealthy businessman trained his mind and body to become Batman, hoping to rid Gotham City of evildoers.

Commissioner James Gordon: head of the Gotham City Police Department and a loyal friend of the Dark Knight.

Edward Nygma: also known as the Riddler, this Gotham City super-villain wields a question-mark cane and a clever tongue.

Gotham City: Bruce Wayne's hometown.

Oswald Cobblepot: sometimes the mayor of Gotham City, but always known to Batman as the Penguin, a mastermind of the city's criminal underworld.

Ra's al Ghul: a centuries-old villain who hopes to save the world by killing most of humanity and ruling the few people who remain.

Society of Shadows: an organization of highly trained assassins led by Ra's al Ghul.

VISUAL QUESTIONS & PROMPTS

1. Batman often uses high-tech devices while solving crimes, including radio sunglasses [at right]. Identify two other panels in which Batman uses one of his high-tech gadgets. Describe them and write about how these devices could be useful in fighting crime.

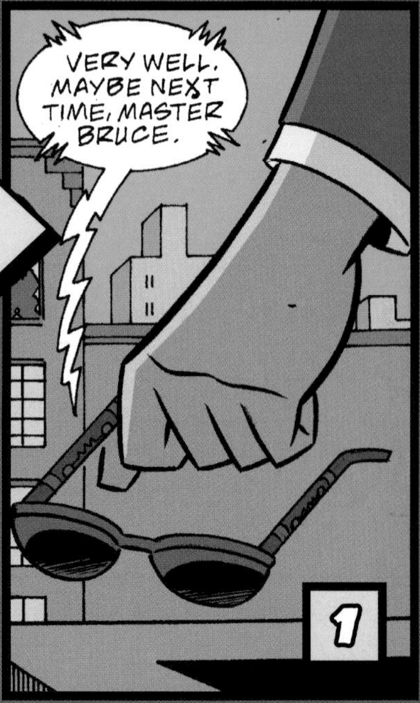

VERY WELL. MAYBE NEXT TIME, MASTER BRUCE.
1

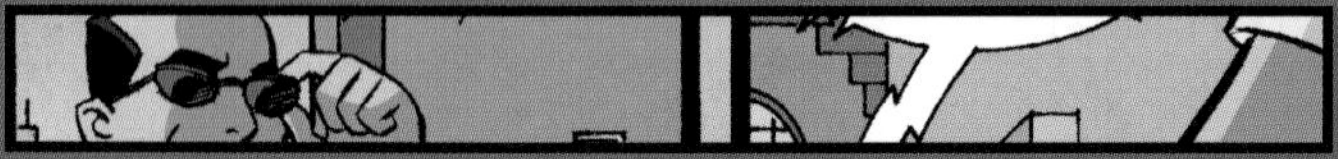

2. In comic books, speech balloons don't always contain words. Some contain symbols or punctuation marks. Each panel below contains a wordless speech balloon. What do you think those characters are saying or feeling? Explain your answer.

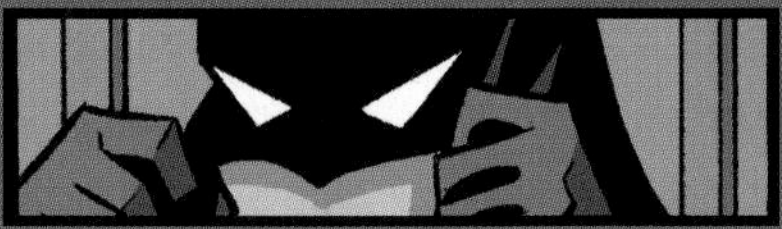

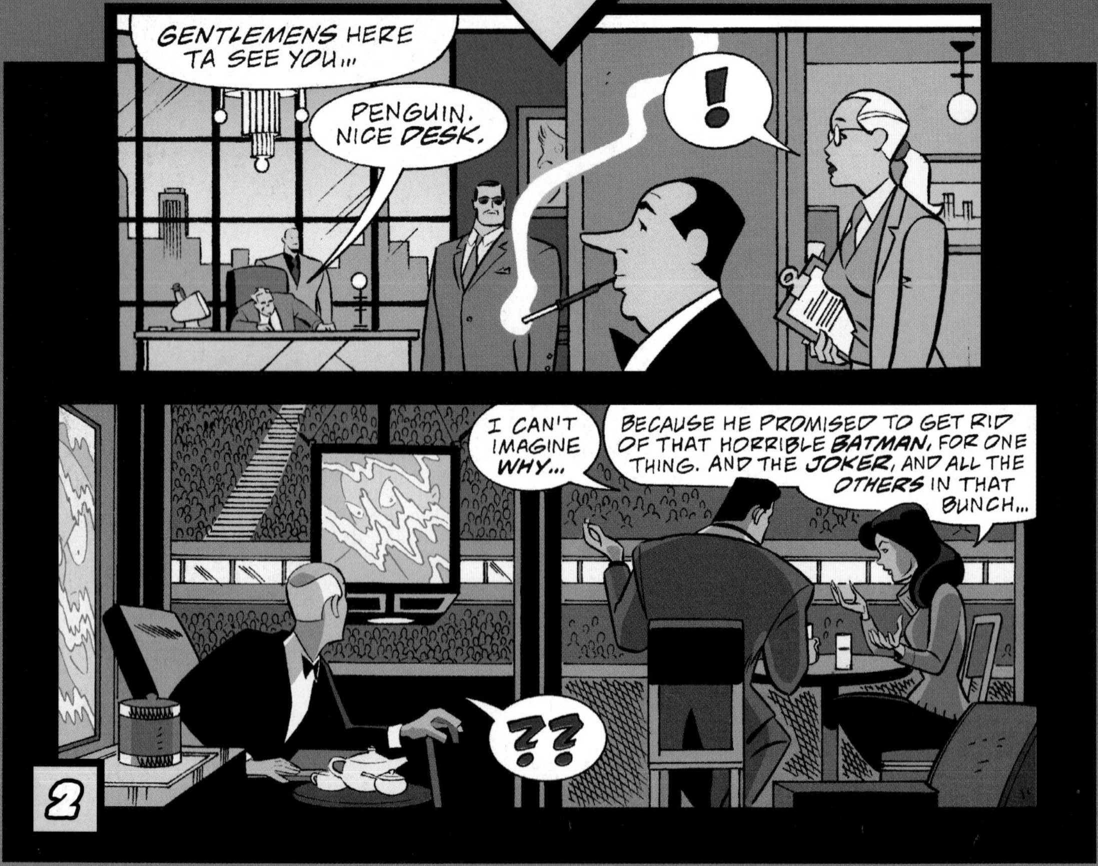

GENTLEMENS HERE TA SEE YOU...
PENGUIN. NICE DESK.
!
I CAN'T IMAGINE WHY...
BECAUSE HE PROMISED TO GET RID OF THAT HORRIBLE BATMAN, FOR ONE THING. AND THE JOKER, AND ALL THE OTHERS IN THAT BUNCH...
??
2

3. Super heroes and other comic book characters often have distinctive features. Batman can be recognized by his eyes alone. Name at least three other distinctive physical features of the Dark Knight. Why are these features important?

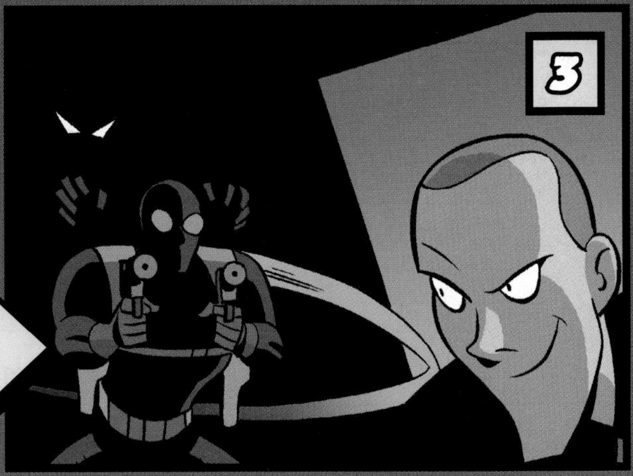
3

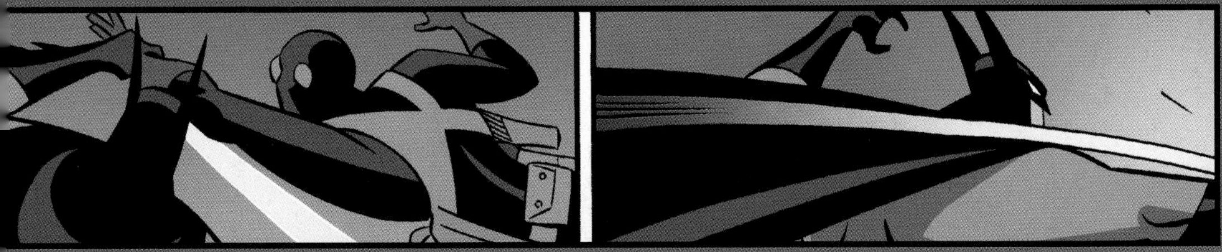

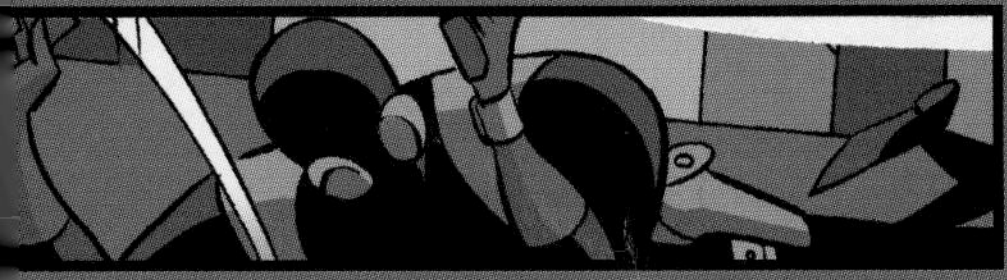

4. Comic book artists often use symbols to show how a character is feeling. In the panel at right, what do you think the symbols above Batman's head mean? How did you come to this conclusion? If needed, look back at the story for clues!

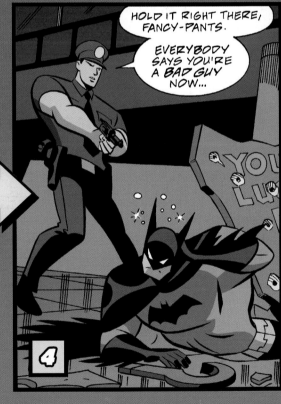

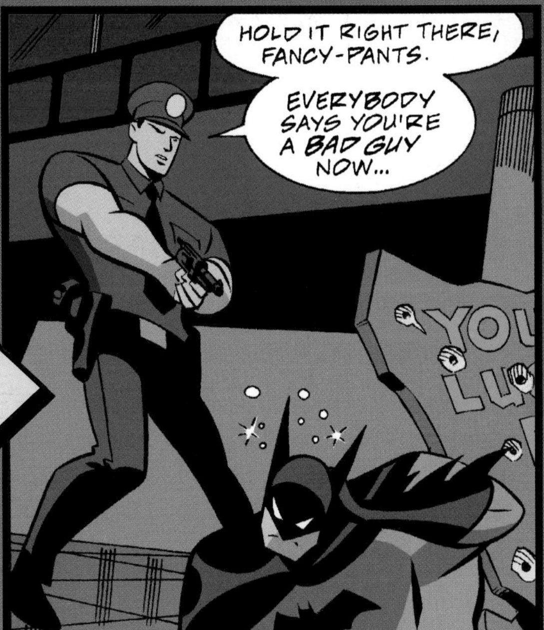
HOLD IT RIGHT THERE, FANCY-PANTS.
EVERYBODY SAYS YOU'RE A BAD GUY NOW...
4

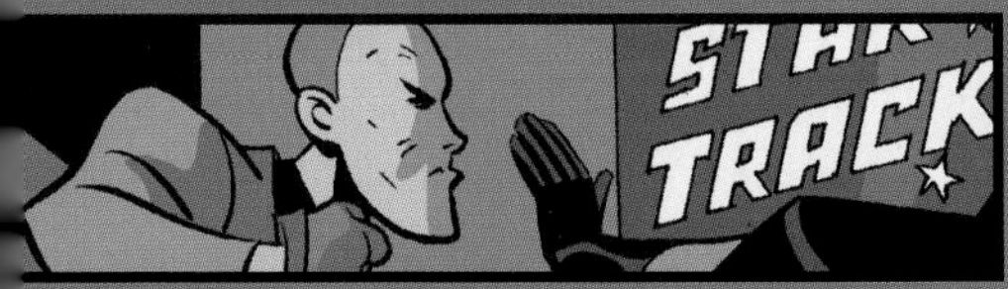
TRACK

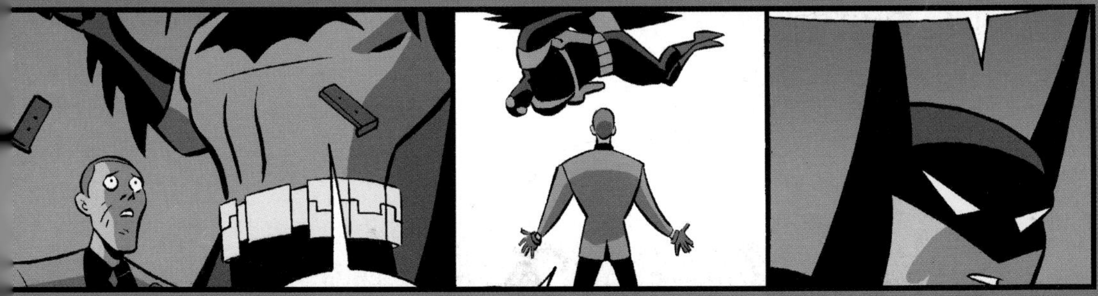

BATMAN ADVENTURES

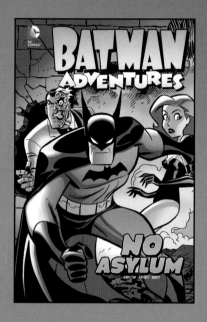

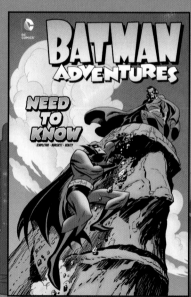